Praise for

Ice Upon a Pier

"Combining a captivating voice and a carefully-built magic world into an intricately plotted story of violence and attraction, *Ice Upon A Pier* is both a compelling queer adaptation of history and the best thing to happen to urban fantasy in years**.**"

—**Brendan Williams-Childs,** *featured in Best American Mystery and Suspense of 2022*

"Gritty, clever, and full of tragedy and unexpected warmth, Ladz carefully weaves a story that melts your heart as it ices the rest of you over. You do not want to miss this."

—**Ezra Arndt,** *editor of MY SAY IN THE MATTER*

"In *Ice Upon A Pier*, Ladz sets bare the beating, albeit slowly, heart of their lesbian ice magic assassin with both clinical true crime precision and piercing pathos giving us a character doomed from birth but still defiantly set upon a path to change their stars . . . . one frozen corpse at a time."

—**Jordan Shiveley,** *HOT SINGLES IN YOUR AREA*

"A dark and dirty neo-noir that throws a one-two punch of a lived-in fantasy world and a compelling hook that keeps you turning the pages."

—**Magen Cubed**, *author of LEATHER & LACE*

"I read this urban fantasy told in the style of true crime in one sitting. Centering a voicy lesbian assassin, this novella pulls no punches on the cyclical relationship between trauma and violence while honoring queer rage and autonomy."

—**Naseem Jamnia**, *author of THE BRUISING OF QILWA*

"You had me at *ice-magic-using lesbian contract killers in a secondary world reimagining of the tri-state area*!!!"

—**Sam J. Miller**, *author of THE BLADE BETWEEN and BOYS, BEASTS, & MEN*

"A gritty journey into the life and times of a sapphic ice mage assassin, *Ice Upon A Pier* is what noir fantasy should be: dark, layered and endlessly compelling."

—**Victor Manibo**, *author of THE SLEEPLESS*

Ice Upon a Pier

Ladz

Robot Dinosaur Press

Robot Dinosaur Press is a trademark of Chipped Cup Collective.
www.robotdinosaurpress.com

Ice Upon a Pier

Publication history
First Edition: April 2023

This is a work of fiction. Names, characters, organizations, places, and events portrayed in this work are either products of the author's or authors' imagination or are used fictitiously. Any resemblance to actual persons, living or dead, business establishments, events, or locales is entirely coincidental.

Book Cover by Aleta Perez (https://www.aletaillustration.com/)

ISBN Data
eBook: 979-8-215076-42-2
Paperback: 978-1-949936-65-0

Contents

Content Warnings

Bullying, killing your bully, killing your parents, death of a child (off-page), vomiting, immolation, poisoning, gun violence, and a mention of beastiality. There is a cat, the cat does not die.

To Marcus, Henry, Ben, and everyone at Last Podcast on the Left -
thank you for the brain rot

Introduction

Then

The elevator doors opened, revealing the tallest woman I had ever seen.

Her black hair, streaked with blonde, sat atop her head in two rolls which cascaded into beautiful curls. The dark purple velour suit enhanced slim curves. Cute, buckled heels decorated her dainty feet. She could have been any of the many affluent patrons in this fine-ass hotel, but from the lack of purse and bulges in her pockets, I could tell she wasn't. She was like me—another contract killer for hire.

"Want me to hold this for you?" she called, reaching for the button panel.

"Y-yes." I dashed over to the elevator and slid inside. The doors reopened with a jerk, then closed with a ping.

My stomach dropped as the elevator ascended. *Fuck, fuck, fuck.* Someone put out a hit on me. It was the middle of the night; there shouldn't have been anyone else here. At least, no one else in my line of work. The streets outside were empty, the lobby deserted.

"So, what'cha up to?" she asked, hands crossed over her chest.

"Working." I couldn't give more details than that. I should *not* give more details than that. A hair comes loose from the braided wreath I arranged it in—I tucked it behind my ear.

"Oh, same! Are you a lady of the night?"

I widened my eyes. "No. Yourself?"

"No, though I've always wondered about it." She smirked. "You're here for a mark."

One of the things that made me so good at what I do was never leaving any collateral damage. Potentially being the mark left me no choice. This other hired hand must die.

My jaw tensed, but I didn't respond. Her blank, pleasant face didn't shift.

The elevator dinged when it stopped at her floor. "Relax, you're not mine."

She winked at me and gave a cute wave before leaving to complete her contract.

My heart thundered in my ears, and I'm not entirely sure if it was relief or something else. I've experienced attraction before, but never towards anyone in my line of work. Never towards anyone *active* in my line of work.

In short, I was in danger.

Now

A singular bulb swings softly above myself and the interviewer. I don't have the right kind of magic to snuff it out, but fuck, is it annoying. Makes me feel dizzy and the depravation of proper food and proper water doesn't help nothing.

"So that's how Ruta Pawlak met Frieda Masters." I want to punch this biographer's face. He's *judging* me. As if he wouldn't be turned on and terrified by the tallest woman he had ever seen getting into an elevator with him. On a night where he thought he would be alone. The prick.

"That's how I met Frieda Masters, yeh." I toss the felled strands over my eyes and out of the way. It works, somewhat.

"And how did it make you feel?" Tooth-pick thin lips narrow. At least his posture relaxes.

I have been nothing but cooperative. Handcuffed, I pose him no danger. Drugged for days in the name of psychotherapy, there is no threat from me. Plus, he's been here for several sessions over many weeks, having me talk about my unpleasant past, which only gets more sordid the more details I tell him. We've only really talked about the most recent stuff—my capture, my arrest, the court proceedings, all that nonsense. It's not even the most interesting part.

I raise an eyebrow. "How often do you see two bounty hunters sharing an elevator? I don't think I was...what's the word? Paranoid? Sure. Yeh, that's it. Paranoid. The only reason for her to have been there was to take me out."

"Why did that worry you?"

The guards had taken my rings—thick silver bands that went on my thumb, index, and middle fingers—and wow, do I want to click them against each other. "I wasn't done. I wasn't done at all. I had so many other contracts to fulfill." So many volumes of graphic novels, both domestic and international, to read. The manga imported from abroad are my particular treasures, rotting in storage while I'm jailed indefinitely.

"Done implies that you started." He flips through that annoying notepad of his. "I don't have much on that. Care to get into it?"

I don't *care* in any sense of the word. But I am bored, and if people want to hear my story, then it's good that they hear it directly from me first.

Chapter 1: The Beginning

Before Birth - 12 years old

Then

Pier-Upon-Pier City. My story started the year when the latest and certainly not last of several great wars ended. Immigrants from an ice-laden land appropriately named Lodska came on boats by droves with their ice magic because their government got trampled by every neighboring country. My father came on a ship with his family, and wow, do I still wish the bastard drowned then.

It means I wouldn't be here now, but some sacrifices net positive benefits.

I know nothing of my grandparents, except that they somehow secured a private room in an otherwise over-crowded tenement complex. This was the height of luxury in those days, despite waking up most mornings to fucking rats—both literally and figuratively. Shouts and screams echoed from every other room. My grandparents died before I came into the picture. Their passing made space for the small, blossoming family of that horrible man and that passive woman who consummated something to create me.

My mother cared for me as much as she could. But she couldn't protect me from my father's fists or spells. And she couldn't do anything about the way my skin reacted to everything. See, it wasn't that I had allergies. The air in Pier-Upon-Pier City was just pure poison like that. Not much has changed, unfortunately, but at least they got rid of the smell.

To get me to stop scratching, my father would use his scant magic to freeze the blood beneath my fingertips and tear the nails off. The screaming enraged him, but I was too young to communicate better. He took his overstimulation out on my mother or out on some poor slob in the street.

With how much it seemed he hated his first child, it mesmerized me that my parents had another one. Piotrek, they named him. And the son born after him.

Now, I wanted to kill my father over the fingernails thing. Because wow, why would you do that to your child? What really sealed the nail in the coffin, so to speak, pun fully intended, is what he did to Piotrek. The first one, obviously.

Piotrek complained—a lot. Not that I could blame him. We were four people living in one room. My father's temper accounted for all of ours.

As did his rage.

As did his violence.

Too long would go by before I had the abilities and wherewithal to do anything about it.

———————————— ❄ ————————————

Summer. The air reeked of dirty bodies and the bags of refuse left on street corners for far longer than humanly acceptable. We were all sweating and Piotrek, in particular, did not like being warm.

And our father loved being drunk, which only made him sweatier. *Loved* isn't the right word, but it silenced the demons in his head enough that he could make them our problem. It helped nothing. Headaches and hangovers ignited his temper. My mother was lucky to be working—most women did at that time. It was a matter of survival. Someone in our family had to. That shitty dock job which ruined her back and hands spared her from my father's harm.

In that room, for most days, it was me, Piotrek, and my father—can I call him Simon? Great. Anyway, Simon's morning bender hadn't ended. The trigger was unclear, but from what I know of the motherland, there wasn't a moment in history that didn't lead to some kind of post-traumatic stress. Especially then, but it wasn't as bad as it was going to get.

Simon grumbled under his breath, a wet, gargling sound which had no words I could decipher. Maybe it was Lodskish, I wouldn't know; my parents never taught it to me. But Simon was so loud when I didn't want to hear him.

Especially when I didn't want to hear him.

And Piotrek couldn't stand summer in that apartment either. The heat, the smells, the noise, none of it. Piotrek, however, was stupid in that way all five-year-olds are. He had just learned how to communicate in paragraphs, knew his colors, had the precise words for the things bothering him. Before then, Simon spared him from his own outbursts. I'm sure some of my bad habits are a result of too many knocks to the head. Same goes for my stunted height.

I never saw the worst of it.

It happened while I was at school.

I came home and Piotrek was gone. Not like missing, but dead. I didn't see the body, but my mother's choking weeping said more than words could ever convey.

From what Frieda showed me of her well-adjusted family, this wasn't normal in any way, shape, or form. I still don't understand why she resented them in the way she did.

But the only story I can share is my own. And there it was.

Now

In my own trauma, I repressed what exactly happened. But I freeze, unable to continue. I stare at the metal table, eyes wide. The only sound I hear is the creaking as the light hangs above us. I am elsewhere. If time stopped, it's not because I did anything.

"Can I talk about something else?" I ask. My voice is disgustingly soft. Simon is dead. He cannot hurt me anymore. Some scars do not heal.

"Of course," the biographer says.

So, I turn to a more fun topic, where I had more agency: dealing with hooligans.

Then

If you think school was any easier, well. You're an idiot, and not in the way five-year-olds are. I don't know what to say otherwise.

As a student, I think I did well enough. I can clearly speak and understand what people are telling me, but, more importantly, I understand what people *aren't* telling me. Most of that, however, I learned in my line of work.

School, whether it intended to or not, prepared me for it.

There were plenty of magicians and non-magicians in public schools, but I was the only ice mage in P.S. 65. They called me Glacial. Especially this one kid. Percy Green. He was bigger than me, less of an immigrant—I think his family came over on the first crossing centuries ago. He had it out for me like I personally wronged his family. But that wouldn't make sense; an ocean separated our ancestors and guardians until this moment of childhood.

He annoyed me very much.

His house was between mine and the school. Most days, he followed me, asking if I could go any slower, if I'd be melting because of the sun, regardless the season. Bastard—literally—stayed far enough away from me that I couldn't spin around and thwack him. How I wanted to, every time he opened that grating mouth.

One afternoon, I gave in to those urges. He asked me about my walking speed. My fist curled into a ball. This twelve-year-old girl snapped a punch into Percy Green's freckled face.

Unfortunately, the incident took place too close to his house. Percy's father saw the whole thing through his window. He threw open his door and yelled expletives I can't remember, nor had I heard before that day. I shivered, not because of cold, but anger. If he had known what kind of little shit his son was, then maybe he would understand why I had to clock him.

I didn't realize a crowd had gathered—seeing a grown man yelling at someone else's kid provided enough entertainment, I suppose. Not like there is still anything else to do in that dumpy neighborhood. All I wanted to do was go home and read the true crime rags I loved at the time—still do, really. I wanted to be in my cramped apartment reading.

The one time my father ever came to my side was that afternoon. He left on a beer run when he saw the commotion. Seeing a depraved kindred spirit, Mr. Green was about to explain to Simon what happened. Why he felt justified in harassing a bullied twelve-year-old over fighting back against his shitheel child.

Simon wouldn't have it.

Like father, like child, Simon sucker-punched Mr. Green, knocking him out. Stunned silence surrounded us. I didn't even know how to react, but I wanted to laugh. Not triumphantly, but more at the ridiculousness of Simon coming to my rescue. Simon would have hit me if I cried, so I just left my mouth hanging open.

Even though he spared me from further embarrassment in that one instance, I still hate Simon for what he did to Piotrek.

Anyway, I thought Percy would leave me alone after that. He and his dad had matching broken noses. But this is Pier-Upon-Pier City—Percy wanted revenge.

I used to go to the newsstand after dinner. There was excellent series on true crime and serial killers from a strictly forensic point of view that fascinated me. It put science to practicality in a way that made it more salient than school ever could.

On my way back, however, Percy called my name. Or rather, he called that gratuitous nickname he had for me. *Glacial*. When he came up with the nickname, I hadn't even awakened my ice magic yet. But it came with puberty. To add insult to injury, my period had started that morning, with all its fun discomforts. Ice flowed through my veins, pricking at my fingers, waiting to be unleashed. Meanwhile, my stomach roiled and my lower back cramped. Fuck, I was uncomfortable.

In hindsight, no wonder I so easily punched the little shit.

"Can I help you?" I responded, calmly. I wasn't going to start the fight. Instead, I tucked the magazines I bought under my arm, ready to go home without incident.

"All alone, huh?" Percy rolled his sleeves up. "Good. My nose still hurts, you fucking iceberg."

Iceberg was a new one. My jaw twitched. I had enough of this kid.

Percy, large in his father's over-sized coat, like some kind of predator, stomped towards me. His fists were ready. He wanted to break my skin and make sure I carried the scars until the end of my days. Or I wouldn't even have the chance to form scars, because I would be dead that night.

The problem with bullies, however, is that they are never prepared for their victims to fight back.

He charged at me, loudly. Knowing his play, I ducked out of the way. Ice crystals formed in my mind, their perfect structure coalescing into smooth, cold cerulean. They materialized on my free hand. I curled my fingers into my own frigid fist and hit Percy.

Again.

Again.

And again.

Now

"And you didn't get caught?" the biographer asks. His breath quakes. I guess me at twelve was kind of scary.

I laugh, this ugly barking sound. "I wouldn't be here with you right now if I got caught."

He tilts his head from side to side. "I suppose you're right." Though his words are uncertain, he recovers quickly from his fear. Not a new wrinkle forms on that face.

"You said at our last session that it's not like they can give me more life sentences." I chuckle; it's a good reminder. I can tell him whatever I want, however many times he tries to visit.

He swallows hard. "What did you do to Percy?"

"He died." I leave it there. It's cumbersome to tell him how I dragged him into the woods, froze off his teeth, fingers, and toes. I took that hideous coat and into the river he went. Oh right, I also weighed him down with rocks. Somewhere in the ocean that body lays. His parents skipped town after that. I'm not sure I ever felt as powerful as I did as a twelve-year-old.

Maybe the biographer and I can have a whole session that's only about hiding bodies and getting away with so much bloodshed. But, fuck, does he annoy me.

It helps him that my hands are locked behind this chair. It saves him that the guards slip magic suppressant into everything I consume. I haven't summoned ice in several years. Shame, because it is beautiful. It solves problems words can't.

And this biographer is turning into a giant fucking problem.

What I Don't Tell the Biographer - At School

As far as whatever publication this man is putting out about me, there are some things I'd rather keep to myself. Here we are.

It is common knowledge that elemental magic happens randomly. Some call it a mutation; others call it a miracle. I call it a tool. Ice served me well. It helped me do what needed to be done to survive, and by survive, I mean get paid.

Myself and the other elementalists formed a little cohort. Percy's disappearance opened up my social circle. Before, people avoided me because they did not want to be on the receiving end of that harassment. With the threat gone, I was approachable. I'm glad I opened up those social doors for them.

It shouldn't have been up to me. But Percy shouldn't have been such a colossal dick.

The unfortunate lesson I gleaned from my school days is this: killing solves problems.

Snuffing out life means that those problems go away. Permanently. And if you're clever about it, no one needs to know.

And wow, was I clever.

Chapter 2: The First Contract

Nineteen years old

Now

Several days pass, but we're back in the same conversational cell, just me and that biographer.

"Tell me about your first job." This statement from the biographer seems so simple, I laugh.

"Is that all there is? 'Tell you?'" I click my tongue against my teeth in that way to let the guards know I'm thirsty. These sessions have been the most I talked in years.

"You and Ten Pan worked together for longer than I've heard of any other contractor working with anyone." His pronunciation on 'Pan' is a hate crime. He stretches out that "a" like the man's name rhymes with a kitchen accessory.

"The pay was good, the jobs easy." I shrug. "Isn't that why you keep your job?"

The biographer laughs and it feels like nails on the metal table separating us. "I'm chuckling because you're right. Good pay and work that feels easy."

"Is there anything I can do to make this job harder?" I genuinely want to know.

He shrugs. "I won't be answering that. These sessions are about you, anyway."

I hate when things are about me. "If you want to know about Ten *Pan*, then why have me start with Frieda?"

"Pardon, but I think *you* started with Frieda."

"Then you need to ask better questions." *Annoying, annoying, annoying.*

Then

You wouldn't think that the Syndicates deal with contracts and blood pacts, but in fact, they do—just like any other proper job. At least, from what my mother told me. Even the docks required documentation to work there, though, and more often than not those contract were scratch sheets with a start date and a signature. Enough to verify employment in those times, not so much now.

Between finishing high school and my first contract with Ten Pan, petty crime sustained me. My parents didn't care in the classical sense. When I came home one night with a whole bunch of comics and manga I certainly didn't pay for, my mother turned a blind eye and Simon lay passed out on a chair in a bib of his own vomit. It had gotten that bad, and no one who lived in that small room knew how to deal with it. Telling him to clean up after himself or stop drinking altogether only upset him more.

As for the second son named Piotrek, Mother used all her savings—which I didn't realize we had—to send him off to boarding school somewhere in the mountains. You know, those states so small, you wonder why they don't just combine into one larger structure. I'm not a historian; I'm sure there were reasons for it.

I didn't get to speak to my new brother during our respective childhoods. Given how everything turned out, it was probably better for the both of us.

Anyway, my first job.

Members of one Syndicate loved nothing more than fucking with members of other Syndicates. It's absurd, really. Half the available jobs boiled down to increasingly violent pranks. Ten Pan had a sister, whom he referred to as Ta Pani (her real first name was Gosia). To survive, she recommended keeping a personal code. Or if not a code, a set of rules about my own boundaries when it came to violence.

I hadn't thought about it before. But I landed on no children and no killing parents in front of children. Drawing the line somewhere ensured an easier time killing, or something. In the Syndicates, no one cared about your conscience except you. It was my choice to care and maintain some facsimile of professionalism for my own self-esteem.

I also decided that I didn't want to spend any time with them beyond negotiations and jobs. Church and state or something, but this pathetic mega-continent didn't do so well at that itself.

Where did I spend all my time, you ask? In illustrated stories with crisp lines and brief dialogues from a country I never had any aspirations to visit.

In fact, after my arrest, I had to arrange to store my entire manga collection because there's only room for so many tomes in our personal prison cubbies. You likely didn't get to see my apartment, but it was filled floor-to-ceiling with various collections, series, and arcs. If I actually cared to have people over, I probably would have hit some world record. If I couldn't spend these ridiculous earnings on images and stories that made me see something even a few feet beyond myself, what was the point?

Lives are cheap and temporary; art is priceless and eternal. And I wanted to fund my own piece of immortality.

The displeasure of a break-up eluded me my whole life. Ten Pan, however, had a rolodex of exes. Some belong to the Syndicates, others kept as far away from the underworld as possible.

The ex he had in mind for my target—George Ubogski—belonged to another Syndicate. No, I won't name the Syndicate, but I'm sure you can figure it out based on all that sweet, sweet, public knowledge of my victims. He made himself too easy to follow, but I'm not going to victim blame because honestly: I am clever.

There are a few details I need to establish about winter in Pier-Upon-Pier City. It never lingered. The seasons cycle from summer's oppressive soup-air to a pleasant, chilled breeze. This lasts for a few days, maybe weeks if you're lucky. Then the rain starts. The temperature dips and plateaus, but it never got cold enough for snow to stick or for blizzards to come, though there have been a few great s torms.

This is the fanciest way to say: black ice is not uncommon in Pier-Upon-Pier City.

Those skilled enough behind the wheel, however, know how to avoid it. Those lucky enough to be impeded, however, struggle and risk their lives unnecessarily. No trip is so important to ignore the tenets of highway safety.

And because I did not want to be caught in the same circles as anyone in any Syndicate, I had to get to George with my own skills and ingenuity.

The key to a successful hit is research and patience.

You cannot rush these things, which might be true for many other projects, but I wouldn't know. The job I held on a part-time basis involved working as a cashier at a bookstore. I did it for the sweet, sweet discounts. This was during a time when the background check relied mostly on benefit of the doubt that people in need of a job weren't felons or criminals. My first kill was technically an accident in self-defense. Without a last name and with my own silence, no one knew to ask about it.

Times sure have changed.

By some divine providence, George stepped into the shop I worked at. It was the kind of place with cameras at the cash register in case of robberies. The register even had a panic button that summoned law enforcement, though I didn't see us selling anything deserving such a security measure. (I visited a few years ago because I needed to update my collection—they still don't sell anything warranting a panic button.)

I minded my own business, sorting receipts, checking customers out. Until one came in whom I recognized from my contract: George himself.

Now, I don't have the right disposition to be judging men, however, I truly did not understand what Ten Pan saw in this one. He had pieced brown curls in the early stages of unfortunate hair loss. A well-manicured mustache hung heavily on his upper lip with eyebrows to match. A large man, but fit, with pale muscles bulging from beneath the sleeves of a pale-yellow collared tee. Blue eyes hid behind aviator frames.

I normally didn't make small talk. I especially didn't want to know about the day of a man who I was supposed to murder sooner rather than later.

Our transaction was just that. He gave me money; I gave him a bag with his purchases. He left the store.

"Give me a second," I told my coworker. "I have to use the bathroom."

They asked me no questions. I don't remember their name or anything. I don't think we ever interacted on that level. The only thing I wanted from employment was enough income to get me to the next illegal contract. No small talk happened at or around me.

Luckily for me, the bookstore kept the bathroom near the entrance. Nothing looked suspicious as I tried to get a glance at George. What kind of car did that Syndicate dweeb drive? I lacked the kind of keen eyesight to remember the license plate number.

The most ridiculous part about the Syndicates is this: they all lived within walking distance with each other. They had their little territories where they didn't live. Those places were marked unnecessarily as dangerous, even in the daylight, because of a few angry douchebags high on their own perceptions of power.

For all my disdain for the Syndicates, I had little desire to solve that problem. It ran too deep. If we didn't want extralegal groups with their own ideas of justice and enforcement, perhaps this great continent of Benedicta shouldn't have made booze a pariah at the whims of fragile housewives. The country had enough problems, but I'm not smart enough to speak to those.

To hunt George, I knew I had to have a conversation with Ten Pan. He met me at one of the several restaurants acting as fronts. Money had to be laundered somehow.

The bastard got dressed up in a crisp, white suit for the occasion. My only interactions with him thus far included that god-awful uniform I thought Lodskish immigrants grew out of eventually. You know the one: closed-cropped hair gelled forward into a triangle, a shitty goatee, cigarettes, and that tracksuit—either with three stripes or some luxury logo taking up the entire back. The hair and cigarettes remained, and Ten Pan didn't figure out that you still needed to wear some kind of shirt underneath the jacket. It looked nice on him, to the extent that I could admit it.

I arranged my brown hair in what would become my signature braid-wreath. It would take a few more contracts before I acquired the sapphire-blue ensemble which became my work uniform. The silver bands were a gift to myself, one each for my thumb, index, and middle fingers. The clicking soothed my racing brain in times of stress.

The restaurant belonged to his grandmother, a sweet, stooped woman in a kerchief who didn't speak Benedictan. It had wooden chairs with white tablecloths covered by another layer of quilts which didn't match anywhere. Iron lanterns hang off the wooden beams covering the walls and the wooden columns holding up the ceilings. I was told it was a style of the old country, but I had no point of reference.

A menu didn't exist; Ten Pan ordered with the wave of his hand, a bark of the scant food phrases he knew, and in no time, we had a plate each of cabbage-wrapped meat parcels smothered in tomato sauce. His grandmother also brought out twin glasses of red wine and sparkling water.

I shouldn't be so weird about Ten Pan not knowing the language. Simon and Mother didn't teach it to either me or Piotrek. My younger brother, however, found higher education that did instruct him in the language and the culture. There's a lot of beauty to be found in it. I never stopped wondering if, had I turned out differently, I would be afforded such pursuits. He sought it out himself, so I wanted to know where he found out motivation in the first place. Definitely not from our p arents.

Perhaps it's because of that boarding school that took him in, lucky bitch.

"So, tell me, Icy. What can I do you for?" The fact that we had interacted only a handful of times and he already had a frost-related nickname for me made my skin crawl.

"He came into my bookshop," I said, sneering. Under the table, I scissored my fingers, clicking the rings together. I didn't touch the water. I didn't touch the wine. Not unless he did, but there was no guarantee that these liquids came out of the same bottles.

Ten Pan started eating and didn't keel over. It took him the time it takes to chew and swallow an entire roll to figure out who I meant. " *Oh*. Oh, well, plenty of people shop for books, eh?"

"I guess." I scraped up some sauce onto each bite of my own.

"Hmmmm." He slurped up his meal and leaned backward in his chair. Somehow, his white track suit stayed clean. "You think you're set up."

I blinked, trying to remain still.

"You really are frozen, aren't you? Okay, here's a tip from employee to contractor." Ten Pan leaned forward across the table. I did not move. I didn't want to be anywhere near his wine-steeped breath.

"Carry yourself as if someone is always out to get a hit on you, but don't let anyone know. It's pathetic. You'll get got that way."

I pursed my lips and nodded. "All right."

"Anyway, no one knows who you are. I just call you the other Lod, but that could be anyone."

I'd have much rather him call me Iceberg or Glacial—anything but fucking Lod. I wasn't going to argue with him about what pejoratives he could use, but I let the annoyance simmer.

"I'll take it." I took my time cutting the parcels into bite-size pieces like I had always seen my mother do. "So, which of the Syndicate neighborhoods does this target live in?"

Ten Pan swallowed hard. "You're not going to attack him in his house, are you?"

"I'm not a fucking idiot, no."

"Oh, well. Eh, I guess I'll tell you. The information will cost you a b it."

I just needed to make rent for the season. The current sum covered my rent for half a year. "Thank you."

"No, thank *you*. George has been a problem for a little while. Glad to be rid of him."

———————————— ❄ ————————————

The Syndicate neighborhoods are idyllic. There is one in every borough of New Harbor, each one almost suburb-like in appearance. I found myself in the swanky Viridyke district within Outfort, the largest borough. Each house sat a few paces from the one beside it. Intricate gardens with withered plants crushed from alternating cycles of frost and melt decorated the balconies and walkways. Garish statues and modern art sculptures took the place of natural beauty.

With my earnings from this nasty career, I lived comfortably, but not with this level of truly disposable income. I had a bed to sleep on, a kitchen seldom used, and a living room which mostly doubled as a library for my extensive graphic novel and manga collection.

At the time, I had the car I had—don't ask me about the make and model—but it wouldn't blend in. I remember one weekend, after that dinner with Ten Pan, I had it polished and cleaned and buffed to as-good-as-new perfection. It wouldn't be enough to hide how dinky a ride it was. Someone better versed in vehicles would immediately recognize it for the scrap metal it was. No, if I wanted to blend in there, I'd have to be more indirect.

So, I found a gig delivering newspapers. Sure, it was weird for a non-teen to apply to the position, but no one wanted to go to that neighborhood or let their kids go there. It was one of the safer places because all the monsters lived in Viridyke and didn't fuck with each other. If people went "missing," it's because those metaphorical beasts saw the opportunity for immediate financial upheaval and fucked up fantastically.

Coincidentally, I liked that newspaper delivery job. It paid all right. It paid almost as well as the bookshop, but with even less responsibility.

My primary employer, however, was Ten Pan. What was nice about working for him was the lack of deadlines. His moods came in waves, and by the time he organized enough to deal with his rage, bloodlust, revenge, or whatever negative feeling, he had instructions and a very hefty sum to go along with whatever would bring him peace. Temporary peace, but satiety, nonetheless.

George, however, broke his heart. And stole his money. And kicked him out of the apartment they shared—which Ten Pan paid for—and subsequently declared himself the cat's owner. It was the kind of pain that wouldn't just go away.

Apparently, Ten Pan really just wanted the cat back. For years, I wondered why he didn't just hire a crew to get the fluffy fella back, but it turns out heists for living things proved more effort than worth and put the creature's life at unnecessary risk.

I understood that calculation. Sometimes, it just isn't worth it, no matter how cute the prize. He showed me a picture of the cat. It was a perfect loaf of marmalade named Tangelo. I hadn't the heart for pets, but looking upon it, I understood the deep desire for protection.

Ten Pan even offered to pay me more because of that sentimental connection. I never said no to more money. Even with the penalty that came with him tipping me off about George's whereabouts, the payout proved more than satisfactory.

Sunlight streamed through a cloudy, winter sky. In its brightness, scant snow melted. I was on my bike with a messenger bag full of newspapers, each one smooth and wrapped in plastic. Snow fell the evening before, but in New Harbor fashion, melted before noon. I had to be careful on my bike. Any slip could mean my demise. Black ice could be anywhere. Though I commanded it as my element, it doesn't make itself known to me. It's not that kind of relationship, and I never had it in me to get any formal training.

Can you imagine how unstoppable I would be if I had?

George emerged from his home. It's simpler than the others—I later learned that rank in the Syndicate could be easily correlated with the quality of home. He was new money or recently "made" and thus lived modestly compared to those around him. He dressed in grocery-store casual: sweats and a too-large tee shirt overlaid with a puffy coat. Like the asshole he reportedly was, he wore flip flops. In the winter. But he was planning to go from inside to vehicle to inside again and back, so perhaps frostbite wasn't an actual hazard.

His car was also a convertible. It was black with a brown accordion for the roof. The figure on the car's hood was an eagle, not unlike the Benedicta national symbol. Tacky as all fuck. I wanted to car to die with him.

That's when I realize I could make that happen.

I rode in front of him, pretending that I happened upon his car. If only he knew my identity, but I was glad he had no idea what hit him. But a paper courier wasn't unusual. I took full advantage of how common that profession made its face in this area. I veered in front of his car and tossed a newspaper over one of the wrought-iron fences. He honked at me, and I got out of his way.

We approached an intersection. It crossed from one quiet street to another. No other cars occupied the road, which worked for me—no collateral damage. Trees lined the curbs and intersection. What a perfect set-up. I focused my ice magic into my fingertips. One turn would complete my route. To turn, I had to signal, like the good paper courier I was (I only had the job for a few days before disappearing). I left several sheets of black ice, invisible to the naked eye. I carefully made sure they were behind me, and to wobble a bit, as if I had hit some myself. An actor, I wasn't, especially not with props.

George saw me make my turn. What he didn't see were the sheets of black ice I left behind for his convertible to slip and slide on.

He pushed on the gas; I peddled onward. I heard his wheels squeal, and I stopped, waiting for the violent crash to follow.

The crunching of metal against wood brought my heart satisfaction. Those at home in that quiet Viridyke street left their abodes to see the accident. Most of them were older housewives in smoking robes and house slippers, some others wore jeans and sweaters. Upon seeing the wreck, one or two women screamed.

And that's how my first contract died in a car accident of my own making. Eh, that's a lie. He lost control of his vehicle and slammed into a tree. But he never found out what caused his wheels to spin out.

Vehicular manslaughter is a nasty business. Loud, smoking, glass everywhere. Too many witnesses wondering if the person behind the wheel was all right. They were never all right. As in life, so in death, and all that. Especially for George, whose head caved in between the concertinaed hood and the air bag's eruption. I turned my bike around, leaving the gathered crowd behind.

The entire neighborhood breathed a sigh of relief. That peace only lasted until Ten Pan and his crew took over a month later. Then the troubles started again, and Ten Pan quickly snuffed them out. I had nothing to do with their execution. Guilt made itself known only once, and it made me wonder if I did the right thing taking the money.

The exquisite quality of the entire completed series I purchased and read over three days without stopping said, yes. It was all worth it.

Ten Pan even found himself reunited with Tangelo, and I didn't hear from him for weeks except for him showing me a printed album of two dozen pictures of him cuddling that precious feline.

Now

"It sounds to me like you and Ten Pan became friends," the biographer says, slurping out of his mug.

I raise my brows and swallow back a terrible, barking laugh. I have no desire to tell him the full story of my true first job, but this little anecdote did well enough.

This actual first contract, however, needs to be recorded because it's a good story. You don't get to a kill count of between fifteen and two hundred by focusing only on the handful that landed me in prison and granted me my life sentences. That nitwit doesn't deserve to hear that good of a story, and I'm tired of talking to him, anyway.

Chapter 3: The First Job

Eighteen Years Old

What I Didn't Tell the Biographer - How I Got Started with the Syndicates

My warped sense of morality embarrasses me.

The convicts around me have clear reasons for their crimes. They're not all violent, either, which goes to show how fucked up this country of the free is. It's full of arbitrary and arbitrarily enforced rules to subjugate others. I never studied the law outside of learning the various ways the Syndicate members kept out of jail. At the end of the day, however, money rules more powerfully than fear.

Because of my mistakes, I have no currency to exchange.

That isn't to say that this frigid bitch couldn't be persuaded. After all, I had to sustain myself somehow. I don't even remember how I heard about it, but notorious Syndicate manager Ten Pan offered a pretty sum for trying out a new "problem solver," as he called it. This one wasn't bound in paperwork, so it wouldn't be considered my first professional kill. *I* consider it professional—I got paid, after all.

Petty crimes are one way to be put away for life. Low risks make a person sloppy. High stakes, however, keep most people involved safe. Makes some of them happy.

Syndicate higher-ups are no exception.

The only image people knew of Ten Pan at that time was that mugshot from when he got into a fist fight with the wrong "made man" at a very popular pool hall. Idiot. Fights like that should be held in private, but I didn't dictate his life. He was handsome enough before that. He had cheekbones that could cut glass and a chin you could wedge lemon slices into. The orange tan was terrible, but it wasn't anything basic color correction couldn't fix as far as pictures went.

It was also the style at the time.

Unlike his namesake, he had distinct periods of rest and feral activity, like an animal. No time for contemplation or planning, you know the type. He gets his fill of terror and violence and then he sleeps it off for months. As close as we were professionally, I had no idea what he did during hibernation. I didn't offer to guess either—rumors were not how I kept myself safe. The rumors told about me, however, are a story I'm getting into later.

As with all things related to the city's network of Syndicates, the location of that first meeting was painfully vague. They didn't want the authorities on their trail, and they didn't want just any asshole wandering in and getting themselves mixed up in nonsense they didn't understand.

Being dangerous meant being cagey in order to avoid a cage in real life.

Ten Pan is taller in person, but far less intimidating. Stories make the man—or any person, really—and his were all fables. He was not a boogeyman born out of darkened alleyways or from too-bright nights. He was a *man*—he did not scare me, especially not in that purple, three-striped tracksuit.

Nine others arrived that summer evening in a basement beneath a warehouse. It smelled of fish. You could hear the river lapping the walls on the other side. There were no windows.

I don't remember many of the others' details from that night, but I do remember they were all older and thought they had no other options except for crime. I happened to be good at the petty stuff. I wanted an upgrade. Less work, more money, and a tightly run operation where I didn't have to worry about getting caught unless I blabbed.

"Tell me, what kind of jobs are you used to working?" His Lodskish accent was thick as the northern ice pack. I later learned that it was exaggerated—he had as little connection to the motherland as I did.

I grunted, ignoring my diminutive stature. "Petty theft. Scaremongering. Things like that."

"Murder?" He flashed me a silver tooth.

I shrugged. "Sure." I left it ambiguous. He could figure out for himself if I meant that I'd done it before or that it wasn't beneath me. I never told him which of those was true.

He turned to the person beside me, asked the same questions. Then to the person beside them. It went on like this until all ten of us were interviewed. I almost fell asleep. Boredom is the mind-killer.

"All right. You." Ten Pan pointed at me.

I tilted my delicate chin. Adolescence sharpened my curves and reined in my emotions. "Yes, sir?"

"You're going to put out a hit for me." He smiled with his disgusting mug. If any face needed a fist, it was his. "You got any special skills I need to know about?"

Instead, I lifted my hand and concentrated my ice magic into the shape of a sharp stake. "Ice mage."

A twisted grin contorted Ten Pan's face into a villain's. "Wow, excellent. Yes, you are definitely going to be the one for this job."

"Go on, tell me about it." I flipped the brown fringe obscuring the left half of my face. "What's the pay?"

"Seventy thousand." He went to his desk on the far side of that basement.

The others gasped. I didn't. I suddenly realized I had no idea the value of a life. I glanced at the other people standing in a row beside me. One of them raised his bushy eyebrows and gave me a thumbs up. I pursed my lips and nodded to him, then to Ten Pan.

Ten Pan gave me a manila folder with pictures and a small profile inside. "This is the mark?" I asked.

"The man's a bastard. Not literally. Read for yourself."

I do not want to repeat the details of this man's crimes, but he was a menace to livestock and anyone who menstruates. They called him a vampire, but the last one of those was killed decades ago. You can see its teeth in a museum somewhere. But this man's behavior came close to that of the mythic beast.

"He sure is," I said to Ten Pan upon my cursory review. "I'll take the job."

"Bring back a token and I'll give you pay."

I raised an eyebrow. "A token?"

"Trophy, whatever word you want to use. Just bring me proof that he is dealt with."

"You've got it, sir." I didn't know where to start aside from a name and justification in the form of a litany of crimes.

Paper trails purposefully endangered others most of the time, but all records of vampire slaying had been hidden from public access. For some of them, you needed to be part of the academic theater, and I just didn't have that kind of money. Plus, I didn't need anyone on my tail wondering about my article searches.

Once in passing, I asked Frieda if she ever took out something supernatural like that. She laughed so hard, she cried. I never did find out, as was the tendency with her.

Ten Pan gave me an address and the neighborhoods the target frequents most often. My target's name was Christopher Taylor, and he lived in Quay Crag. He enjoyed long walks in the neighborhood. I hadn't spent much time in the borough of Outfort before—little did I know, it would be my primary haunt. It's a quaint little area, especially after sundown when Christopher takes his walks.

This didn't strike me as strange—most people worked from 9am to 5pm. In the summer, the sun takes its sweet time descending the sky. If this guy truly was a vampire, he wouldn't be out until after 8pm. I went with the guess and waited several hours for the last bus out of Pier-Upon-Pier City to New Harbor.

I ate dinner at home, put on gloves, and wore all black, from my tank top to my leggings to my most delicate flats. If I was going to be following someone, I should wear shoes that soften the sounds of my foot falls. Normally, I wore boots, but it was summer, and I couldn't risk being seen or heard.

I blended in with the other young people taking the bus into New Harbor. We crossed the West Gilson River where several get off, disappearing into the night's festivities and dalliances. I transferred to another train and let the rails take me across the East Gilson River deep into Outfort. There was hardly anyone in the car with me, and all I could do was bounce my leg up and down, nervous about this kill.

Possibilities raced through my head like an express train. What if this person truly is a vampire? There are bedtime horrors about vampires and their ilk, how you need silver and holy water. I have neither these things. I didn't believe in them. I assumed my ice magic would be enough. Vampires are, after all, still biological despite being monstrous and undead. Blood needs to flow for them to function, like it is for most living, breathing things.

This assignment was the last time I ever operated on assumptions.

The truth: I was too cowardly to bring weaponry with me. It made me too obvious, and it could lead to problems down the road if I'm not careful cleaning up after myself. Moreover, I didn't need weaponry.

Back when I killed Percy, I only needed what my body provided. I worried for a while that my powers were at their peak in my youth. Oh, am I glad to know they didn't wane as I aged. In fact, they got stronger with use, like a muscle. Sure beat having to shell out money for an air condition in the summer months and ensured that the pipes didn't freeze over in the winter.

My ice magic isn't *all* about murder.

———————— ❄ ————————

I found the home of Christopher Taylor in Quay Crag easily. It was a little more unkempt than the other matching townhouses. Bay windows rolled like hills down the street, with curtains in various states of covering. No one had their lights on except for the city itself in the form of streetlamps and stop lights. Shadows spaced themselves evenly between the orange beams. I had places to hide if I needed them.

Nerves tickled my focus. It's still a heavily residential area, and I, a stranger, was unsure what to do next. I crawled behind a tree and sat on the curb. It was hot and muggy; my face felt like it was melting in a stew of sweat. There was no plan for next steps. But I wanted that money. I wanted large sums of cash in one go so I could fuck off to my studio apartment and read my manga and not worry about work or cashflow for several months.

Or, as it turned out, a few weeks at a time. I lived comfortably enough. The money lasted. But I read too quickly for my own good. Ownership and personal belongings brought their own little joys, and I never wanted to be sad again.

A door closed. My head perked at the sound. I waited patiently until the following footsteps grew faint. My heart pounded in my chest, but no one aside from me seemed to notice my presence. I really *was* going to kill someone for cash. A thought about turning around and forgetting the job slipped past me like a hot breeze. No hesitation.

I rose carefully and faced the direction the squeak of sneakers seemed to be going off to. A lone figure, back turned to me, walked away in the night. There was no one else on the streets, no distant blare of sirens or other signs of a living neighborhood. It was only me and my victim.

Christopher Taylor was as tall as he was beautiful. Pale white skin glistened in the night light underneath a white ribbed tank and loose jeans. Straw-yellow hair flowed from his head, pushed back with a blue headband. The sneakers suggested that he might be out for exercise, rather than some midnight stroll for his living food. This entire vampire rumor clouded my focus. I made a note to stop believing tall ta les.

This *very ordinary man* did not know that I trailed behind him. He shuffled onward. And onward. Turning at random street corners.

He kept me on my toes. My heart rate thrummed like a discotheque's beats the entire way.

We didn't move quickly; it was the most stressful leisurely stroll. I kept a few houses between us, thinking, calculating. It was too hot and any ice I created on the sidewalk would melt immediately and become incredibly conspicuous.

I could just attack him like a feral animal, but those stories belonged to Ten Pan. I didn't want to copy anyone else. I also didn't want to cause a scene and get myself into an irrevocable struggle.

Blood, it occurred to me, was made of water and water freezes. Blood must also freeze. Ice magic tingled at my fingertips.

When I was young, after Percy's death, I tested the limits of my abilities. I pushed myself to fainting in abandoned lots, sneaking out after Simon and Mother went to bed. Piotrek sometimes woke up, crying as babies do. It wasn't my job to soothe him, so I practiced my abilities far away from him.

Do you know how many rodents there are in cities? We are feasts for them. No one notices a few going missing or dying. They eat anything and everything, including each other. Brutal, but horrifying in that way only nature can be.

Humans killing other humans wasn't natural.

Humans killing monsters, however, might be.

I extended my hand, concentrating on the flow of water within the bastard. I had to make this work, to get the temperature within his body to well below water's freezing point—the bits that make blood red means it takes more magical energy to yield the same effect. I stalked slowly behind him, the squeaking of his sneakers obscuring any sounds my soft slips would make. Nighttime had never been so loud.

Christopher slowed his pace, coughing. I maintained my focus, feeling the energy flow into my arms, much like it had during all my practice sessions. There was an awareness that comes with it, an alertness.

And a distorted sense of pride. Ice magic from a frozen land followed me and my family to Benedicta, but I'm the only one of my family who truly harnessed it.

Once his movements slowed, I ducked into a doorway. I dared not lean out, but I could still hear how he walked. It became faint and sporadic. I needed it to stop. This was the most nervous I have ever been on a job. It was going to get me killed if I paranoidly peeked at him from my shoddy hiding spot.

After continuous minutes of use, the expenditure of magic sapped my energy. Weakness, light-headedness, and that comforting feeling of being under a blanket enveloped me at once. I needed to be more careful. I needed to know my limits, but I didn't berate myself for these rookie mistakes until I got home. My body didn't need to be bogged down by the extra stress.

I stopped when it hurt too much. Breathing quietly and pressing my nails into my palms to keep me awake, I waited. There were no more footsteps, just the soft buzz of crickets.

I counted down to three and leaned out. Christopher no longer stood. Instead, he lay prone on the sidewalk. He was still a man. I didn't know what else I expected, but he lay there curled up, as if that would warm him. He had his blood frozen, and I didn't have the energy to keep it that way.

If I left him there, someone would find him. Ten Pan left me no instructions on what to do next, what to do with the body. I breathed in and out as deeply as possible. No one was going to find him; I would make sure of it.

I remembered that the East Gilson River was not so far away. I could just put him in those murky depths. There were bound to be rocks and other landscaping features in the park that could be used to weigh him down.

I crouched beside him. With all the strength in my 5'2" body, I hoisted him over my shoulder like a sack of potatoes. I had to massage him a bit to get that perfect arch for a milk maid's carry, but I managed. A few blocks stood between me and being free of this problem. I would carry the poor sob until then.

Like an ignoramus, it surprised me that his smooth, white skin reminded me more of a chicken pulled out of a fridge than a person who used to be upright. The cold didn't bother my palms, but it bothered my spirit. People shouldn't be that temperature or that stiff. Rigor mortis couldn't have set in. But I had to get over this discomfort if I was going to be earning most of my money this way.

Where this strength and determination came from, I still have no idea. For my best guesses, it stems from magic and the power of youth.

The physical activity cleared my head of the horror that I just killed a person. It was perhaps the last time I experienced shock or regret. All my victims were assholes in one way or another. Am I much better for having taken their lives?

In the line of business I found myself in, trying to divide people into good and bad makes for a terrible thought exercise. How does one judge crimes when, at the end, there's a body either way? Perhaps there is something sinister that I only killed when paid.

It sure felt better than killing for something as fleeting as closure.

———————————— ❄ ————————————

After this tiring adventure, I vowed to never make the mistake of killing my victim so far from the disposal spot. I didn't know if freezing his entire bloodstream would work or if I was delusional. Either way, he didn't stir. There was no heartbeat. He was dead, but he was still a problem.

Sweat poured down my face as the humidity around New Harbor continued to choke the city, despite the sun's nighttime absence. I loathed this part of summer. Granted, I wore all black mostly to blend in and not be too conspicuous, but I could have worn lighter materials. A fool at eighteen, like most newly legal adults. All aesthetic and no common sense.

After what felt like hours when it more likely was one hour in the singular, I found the river. The rusted railing built to deter people from jumping was too tall for me to throw a body over. The water never felt so far away. Benches sat at even intervals looking over New Harbor—it surprised me that the rent in Quay Crag remained so cheap.

No one occupied the seats or the park itself. There were some trees blocking the view between us and the streets. You would have to be looking for mischief to find us. It was a risk. I felt exposed; I wanted this over with.

Momentarily defeated by shoddy landscape architecture, I laid Christopher Taylor down by the rail, the river lapping at the stones beneath us. Panting heavily, I bent at my waist, head pressed into my knees. My muscles ached and the tiredness swept over me like a wave. I should have napped before leaving, done anything resembling preparation before making my way out to Quay Crag. Never again. I filed these mistakes as actions never to repeat.

The sky changed from the darkest blues to the pastels of dawn. So much time had passed, and for what? A half-assed job where a body could still be discovered. I would be put away as soon as I started. No one wanted that failure. *I* didn't want that failure.

To make matters worse, Christopher stirred. Dirt and sidewalk grime got on his white top. Tears pricked my eyes. Fear clasped my tongue. Even dazed, he probably had strength enough to lay me out, even kill me. Then, he would inherit my problem. I didn't want him to have that struggle.

I strategically placed myself behind his line of sight. Pain must surge through his body as he defrosted. He swore several times in succession. He shook his hands and legs, as if that would thaw his blood faster. It might. I tried summoning my ice, but it failed. Either my magic didn't work hard enough, or I didn't have enough within me. But it worked as much as it needed to. He could not move with any kind of agility. Neither could I, but I didn't want to worry about grotesque outcomes when I didn't have to.

Sunlight streaked over the horizon before Christopher had a chance to look at me.

He burst into flame. The sun kissed the New Harbor skyline on the other side of the Gilson. I blocked the rays with my hand raised in front of my face. A billowing plume of smoke and steam rose from his incinerating body. I've never seen anything like it, and I've seen a flaming car wreck a few times in my life. I've never smelled anything like it either. It soured me to the core. I wanted to retch; I wanted to scream as much as the burning man should be screaming. He was perfectly silent aside from fire's crackle. As was I.

Vampire.

The burning lasted for several minutes, much longer than I expected someone to immolate. What remained in the ashes of clothing and flesh was a skeleton. I knelt beside it, hoping it wasn't too hot as to burn through my gloves if I touched it. Two pointed teeth protruding from his skull tempt me. I reached carefully for them. Christopher didn't reanimate.

The skeleton stayed still.

I'm still not strong enough to snap bone, so I took the skull. This person really was a vampire. No wonder Ten Pan offered seventy thousand dollars for an unknown quantity. Unwittingly, he also left me with a list of mistakes to never repeat if I wanted to make a career in the freelance murder business.

Chapter 4: Of Orchids and Poison

Twenty-seven years old

Now

"What do you want to talk about today?" the biographer asks.

"You know, let's take a break from just focusing on me and go on about Frieda." Even though it's been years since she passed, I still think of her with fondness. The way she smelled, that ugly laugh she had, how much taller she was than me—it's all in reverence and fondness. She was also very good at what she did.

"Can I ask why?"

I shrug. "It'd make a really good story. Plus, it's hard to talk about my career without talking about the times we intersected." I can't do the math on how long we were together—I'll leave it up to the biographer to fill in the gaps.

The guards bring me a glass of water to lubricate my throat for the ceaseless talking.

Then

Here is where I recount the most sordid details from my storied career. Where I existed in queer frivolity and villainous abandon. I will not be so careless as to divulge the names and places where my hits happened, but please know that they were plentiful. The money was good. The work was constant.

Sometime after the episode in the elevator, I was out in the far suburbs within Outfort on another hit. Just a small house call in Ceramic Bay because some idiot ruined one of Ten Pan's horses with his sexual appetites. Disgusting. There was not a single member of any Syndicate that I respected, with Ten Pan being an asshole who owned horses despite his city living and with everyone else fucking with him in their specific ways. It never ended.

Unless, that is, Ten Pan paid me to go take care of a problem.

The peace and quiet of that cul-de-sac did not suspect a single thing when a well-dressed woman wearing gloves approached the house. No one called the police or any other authority when I went inside and froze the blood in his brain. He didn't have a chance to scream. He might have winced and gasped as if it were run-of-the-mill brain freeze. But this time, it was permanent.

I left the house without anyone noticing or caring. Another simple job. The guy had no family, and there was enough green space between houses that the corpse smell shouldn't bother the neighbors in the same way it would in an apartment building.

"Mutton, fresh mutton." The jingle reverberated throughout the neighborhood of flat two-story homes. It was summer, people wanted to eat outside, but it seemed strange to me. Who sells mutton out of a food truck?

Frieda Masters, it turned out.

And she had customers. People left their houses with cash in hand. I panicked for a minute. Did they know why I had come? Was this some elaborate hit put out on me by another Syndicate?

I stood awkwardly on the curb, watching the woman I hadn't yet known to be Frieda sell sandwiches and other meals to starving suburbanites. My stomach grumbled. I shouldn't have been hungry, but magical expenditure had its own ways of making itself known. I usually didn't carry much cash beyond what the fare would be back to Pier-Upon-Pier City. As if fate determined it, I had enough money to grab food.

The line wasn't huge, but wow, people got really excited for this fresh mutton.

"What can I get you?" Frieda pushed up the light blue kerchief holding back her black-and-white hair. "Oh, it's you from the other night."

I glanced around me. No one here looked like other boogeyfolk from the Syndicates. "Indeed. Funny we should run into each other again."

"This time, I think you're in my turf." With a friendly wave, Frieda Masters gave me her name.

And I shared mine, then ordered a pita with fresh mutton. The mutton was fine, indeed fresh. Condiments made most meals for me—that stuff never expires. I loved the creamy cucumber sauce and ripe tomatoes. Some kind of providence would have it that I even had enough change for a soda.

I sat on the curb, eating, enjoying the texture and crunch under a summer sun.

When I wasn't stalking, killing, or reading drawn stories, I liked to go out. The lesbians of New Harbor's Central Isle had their haunts. I liked women, and that label suited me best, I think. Men disgusted me, but the more I think about it, the more I realize I never met one that wasn't absolutely reprehensible. Simon couldn't control his temper, Ten Pan sucked in more ways than one, and Piotrek was a brother I spent zero time with. I knew next to nothing about him except for the stuff you can read in an internet biography. All my victims were male. So, no, there were no males to be the targets of my admiration.

Sometimes I would see the kind of man people posted on the covers of magazines. My brain could not compute. I didn't feel those tummy tingles or the dry mouth people talked about.

But when I saw Frieda among the dykes and femmes in Yoked Beyond Reckoning, my body tingled the way it did upon expending my magic. Never having worried before, I swiped a hand over my braids, straightened my blazer, and shuffled my feet.

"Ruta!" Frieda called to me over the music. I think it was synth night, but I couldn't be sure—that bar played such an eclectic mix, I never knew what to expect on any given evening. Plus, music and its discrete genres didn't interest me.

I waved. She grabbed my hand and pulled me into the throng that was half grinding on each other, half swaying, soft bodies pressed against curves shuffling on awkward feet. Holiday lights served as the only lighting. The floor was sticky with the faint smell of beer and sweet liquors. It was not romantic, but it was perfect.

She bought me a drink.

And another. Both a sweet one and a bourbon-based one. A syrupy cherry drew a streak of red in the ginger-flavored cocktail. I liked them. I liked her.

I stopped before a third because I never wanted to find out what I was like in alcohol's sweet oblivion. My father set that precedent, a warning of things to keep in the dark.

For a moment, I worried that my heart would stop on that dance floor because of poison. It didn't.

I had a great night. She invited me to her place somewhere in Outfort. But I was a coward. She kissed me, and I returned to Pier-Upon-Pier City alone.

Since Frieda seemed to be stalking me, I decided to repay her with my own exploration. She frequented lesbian bars which made the search much easier, but I didn't want her in recreation—I wanted her at work.

It was stupid to assume one location extrapolates to general hunting grounds, but I didn't want to interact with Ten Pan when I didn't need any money. I started with Outfort, that massive borough split into several districts, some of which I already made myself somewhat familiar with.

Syndicate families live where they always had. I couldn't find any rhyme or reason around the chosen locations. Outfort wasn't close to the dangers and diversions of Central Isle. Even today, I have mixed feelings on its taming. Gentrification and the police crackdown ruined the city in more ways than one, turning the place into a manufactured habitat for people who confused owning things with having a culture.

I was among the quiet residences of Quay Crag when I heard the call of, "Mutton! Fresh mutton!"

My stomach grumbled like some kind of Pavlovian response, even though I had one of her pita sandwiches only once. Little did I know at the time, I hungered for more. More time with her, more of the sound of her voice, more of her lips on mine—there was so much to want.

I raised my hand and waved. Frieda had her hair in twin braids hanging against her cheeks. She covered her regular clothing with a blue-and-purple checkered apron.

"Hi!" She called. "What can I get you?"

I smiled, pale lips quirking to one side. "Your sandwiches are fantastic. I'd like another."

"You've got it." She disappeared behind the elevated counter and got to work. Meaty, unctuous smells permeated the air. I was surprised it didn't summon a crowd like it did in Ceramic Bay when we met for the second time. More for me, I guess, both in terms of time with her and in terms of snacks.

She emerged a few minutes later. We traded money for a meal.

Before I took a bite, she said. "So, what can I do you for?"

I laughed, licking a bit of sauce from my lips. "What do you mean?"

"You don't live here, and I don't have a newsletter or anything telling you where my truck will be. What's up, Ruta?"

My stomach fluttered at her use of my name. Everyone else used some kind of ice-based nickname. "I'll admit, I was hoping to run into you."

"Wow, same!" She leaned forward, beckoning me closer with a finger. "Want to accompany me on a hit? It's at a hotel in Ceramic Bay."

I raised an eyebrow. "Is that allowed? I mean, doesn't that put you at risk?"

"Not really. I'm just getting dinner with a few soon-to-be-former associates." She didn't tell me any information about the capacity in which she worked with them. Plausible deniability generally worked in my favor; she must have known the same tricks. There was never a good opportunity to ask outright.

"Uh, you sure it wouldn't be weird if I came with you?" I kept eating, resting my elbow into the crook of the other arm. I really wanted her to reassure me that it wouldn't be strange. I wanted her to tell me that she wanted me there with her. There was a magnetism around her wide smile and light-hearted demeanor. I swooned at the decency of her not giving me an icy nickname, though there was no way for her to know that I was an ice mage. I didn't show it to her, not until the very end.

"Not at all! I can introduce you as my girlfriend if that makes you feel better." She gave me that smile, eyes closed.

A furious blush lit up my face. "That...that could work." A girlfriend wasn't something I ever considered wanting, not until she said it.

"You're so precious!" She teased with her inflection.

It didn't fill me with any rage or embarrassment. Instead, it filled me with warmth and tenderness. It was the first time I felt this feeling.

I got in the food truck, heart alight, and we were off to Ceramic Bay.

I sat beside her in the shotgun seat. I watched the streets roll by, their various storefronts and apartment facades blending into each other.

Frieda talked. She mentioned how her fathers were both pharmacists—one of them got into it after he transitioned. The medicines and endocrinology got him into the profession. It took many years to perfect his knowledge, at least enough to pass it onto his daughter.

"What about you? What are your folks like?" At a stop light, she ate a piece of gum, chewing like a cow.

I raised my eyebrows and found a single point to focus on. I wanted to vibrate out of my skin at the question. I've barely thought about Simon and my mother in years, let alone talked about them.

"They're, uh, they never broke any laws." If I started talking about what my father did to the rest of us, I'd never stop screaming.

"So, why'd you get into it?" She slowed our roll as she tries to find the hotel's parking lot.

I shrugged. "It's just good business." The pay far outweighed the difficulty of the jobs I completed, but she knew that. She was in the same line of work.

"You know, you're right. It is good business." She turned around her in her seat. "Want to help me prepare some sandwiches?"

So, we did.

It was an easy process, shaving off the meat from its vertical spit, arranging the crisp vegetables, slathering each pita half with the sauce. I could easily do this at home, but sometimes, you wanted the convenience of another person's feeding. And the company—the company is very nice.

"But here's the important step." Frieda pulled out a small tube of what looked like white powder. It could be cocaine. It could be sugar. I never dabbled.

"What's that?" I asked, reaching for it.

She stopped me. "This is cyanide. It tastes kind of like almonds so it's really easy to hide in food." She opened the cap and sprinkled a bit before smearing on more white sauce. "Plus, it mixes well in water."

"You've been around this block a few times, I see."

"You know it. I can teach you what I know, if you'd like."

I smiled at her. "I'd like that very much."

After that night, my days of being a one-trick glacial pony were over.

———————————— ❄ ————————————

With the associates served their dinner, Frieda and I excused ourselves to the bathroom. We stood, leaning side-by-side against the wall. A hotel room had never felt so small—scratch that, any space had never felt so small.

"What do we do now?" I whispered.

She shrugged. "We wait. It takes a few minutes to kick in." A large watch hung off her wrist, the face of it pointing at the floor. She lifted it to check the time. "It's pretty reliable, made it myself." I couldn't tell if she meant the watch or the cyanide mixture.

I nodded gently. I wanted to know more, but quiet patience took priority. We could talk more later, assuming all went according to plan.

The men's voices were muffled on the other side of the door. Three dudes shouldn't be so loud, but I knew better.

"Fuck, man, my stomach feels terrible." That guttural-voiced associate coughed.

"God, ugh, me too. What the fuck is going on?"

More groaning. I sweat. I was nervous. This energy leaked magic, but I didn't want to create ice. The poison would take care of them, of that I was sure. But I feared that they would burst into the bathroom and it would all be over.

Instead, something else froze—time itself. Frieda leaned awkwardly, mid-exhale. A drop of water hung suspended in the air from the faucet. I didn't know that part of the ice magic permeated everything.

Excitement boiled within me. This new ability would make me unstoppable. I didn't need it, but I wanted to explore in this liminal space between moments.

I snuck out of the bathroom, closing the door behind me. It seemed I could still manipulate anything in my immediate contact. I kept my hands close to me as I walked around the men sitting on the floor, inhaling the cursed sandwiches. Foam formed on their lips. One of their eyes rolled to the back of their head. I had to research the effects of cyanide later—my time-freezing spared me from the minutiae of the more gruesome symptoms.

My eyes widened. It didn't even take five minutes for them to get ill. Soon, they would be dead. And no one would know anything better.

Ice. Poison. Time freezing. There was no reason for me not to become the most powerful contract killer that ever hit Pier-Upon-Pier City and New Harbor.

Feeling the magic slip away from me, I dashed back into the bathroom. At my weakest, time snapped back into its normal cadence.

There was much groaning. One of the lamps fell over. The bulb cracked. Silence. Frieda's skills worked.

"All right, let's check on them." She beamed me an unusually bright smile. She gestured for me to leave the bathroom first. I did, nerves tingling through me as I wondered what lay before us.

The three men in the hotel living room stopped moving. They looked passed out, save for the two that had the foam on their lips. I don't dare touch them; I didn't have my gloves on. I didn't want to leave any evidence of our being there.

Frieda grabbed a sandwich and took a bite. I reached for her in warning. She laughed. "Why are you worried? I am poison. It doesn't affect me." She nodded her head at an untouched wrap. "That's for you."

I blinked at her as if just asked to solve algebra. "Excuse me?"

"You didn't think I'd poison yours too? Who do you take me for?" Her brows knit together in offense. "Oh my God, you're so cute."

She placed a large hand on my head like I was some kind of puppy.

I let out a nervous chuckle. "Look, I just..."

"You're fine! I get it. Can't be too careful. But I assure you, nothing's been done."

The hour got late and neither of us wanted to sleep among dead bodies. She invited me back to her apartment. I didn't want to protest. She lived somewhere in Ceramic Bay, just a few blocks over. Trains didn't run that late, so I accepted her invitation to go home with her.

We held hands as we walked those silent, empty blocks. I didn't deserve serenity. But this felt nice.

Now

"As far as your relationship with Frieda, this all sounds idyllic." The biographer leans back, resting his fingers like a steeple. "It's a bit of a romance, isn't it?"

I shake my head. I've read enough of genre and structure to know that Frieda and I were anything but. "Not at all. It's romantic, sure. But she is dead. I'm in prison. We wouldn't have wound up with that sweet, sweet happily ever after." I swallow; I'm parched and upset. My glass is empty.

I jerk my head towards the guard, who makes a drinking gesture towards his fellows. The door opens, and I get my glass. This time, it has a straw in it.

"Ah yes, the essential of those kinds of stories. I apologize." He flips through his notes. "You know, they initially wanted to catch Frieda on charges of killing those men. But aside from poison, there wasn't much else go on."

I nod. This information is not new to me. Plenty of contract killers used poison. Plenty of others used cyanide specifically. It wasn't her unique trick, but her sharing it with me sure was.

"But she was already gone before they could press charges. They found her dead in her food truck. You wouldn't know anything about that, would you?"

Tears well in my eyes. I didn't think I had any left to spill over Frieda. "Can we talk about something else?"

I need just a little bit longer to process my feelings over that loss. Years weren't enough time.

What I Didn't Tell the Biographer - The Physicality of Me and Frieda

Frieda Masters was a deeply flawed person. She had to slather herself in poison to ensure she had an immunity to her own wares. She laughed so hard, she choked more often than not. Killing people with poison gave her the same kind of pleasure sports gave others. When she talked about her family, there was a bite to her words that didn't become obvious until it was way too late.

But when it was just the two of us, together, not as hired killers but as two women sharing an attraction, she was perfect.

Our absurd size difference did complicate things a bit, definitely at the start. Her being a full foot taller than me meant I had to get on my toes to kiss her because I didn't wear heels. Some women figured out how to run away in them, but that wasn't me. Practical footwear all the time matched my activities. Funnily enough, I never had to run away from a situation. Usually, I stalked away. Or froze time and walked away in that liminal space of my own creation. Never from Frieda, though.

Frieda kissed as if she was drowning.

Frieda ate me out as if my cunt provided the only liquid that could sate her thirst.

Frieda laughed her awful laugh because I kept forgetting which planes of her long frame made her ticklish.

I rested my head on her modest chest as if they were the only pillows which could help me sleep.

I liked her limbs entangling me. It felt safer than my one-bedroom apartment and its several deadbolts.

The number of times I wanted to freeze time when embraced with her is higher than I care to admit. Simply put: I was in love. Yes, the attraction lit a spark like a wildfire, but the passage of time made the relationship so much richer than any fiction I had read.

It was the passage of time and nodes and networks in our lives that enriched this relationship to depths I couldn't have imagined or welcomed for myself. It felt separate from the violence of the rest of my life. The fleeting fears and waves of cashflow.

At least I always had those evenings to hold onto in my cold heart.

Chapter 5: Families

Thirty-five years old

Now

"What would you rather talk about?" the biographer asks.

I slurp my entire water in one gulp. This much talking should be outlawed as cruel and unusual punishment. And yet, the words haven't run out yet. I want to keep going, despite my face's protests. The guard hovers over me, as if I was going to attempt anything ridiculous. I'm sure the water had been drugged with something to suppress my magic. It doesn't leave me with the same headache as other drinks I've had within these four walls. That interests me, but I cannot say anything without rousing suspicion. It's not like the biographer would have any idea anyway—he's a guest, not the e stablishment.

It's strange it's taken me so many sessions to notice the differences.

"Piotrek managed to completely avoid jail," I tell the biographer.

He knits his brows together in confusion and flips through his notes. "Didn't you tell me earlier that he died?"

"Yes, and then two years later, they had another son. They also named him Piotrek." The biographer tenses, and I let out a laugh. "That was my reaction. I was ten years old when he came out of my screaming mother's cunt. Before you ask, Simon was too drunk to drive her to the hospital or call 911. I used my magic to keep her cool in that oppressive summer." That episode inspired me to seek getting my tubes tied as soon as I could. "Sorry I didn't mention him in my account of Percy. Didn't think it mattered."

It matters a lot, actually. Piotrek the second ruined my life, and it matters so much I'd rather not think about it, forget talking about it. The biographer waits for me to continue. He makes no motions to r eply.

I breathe deep. "Simon would leave the house to 'work,' but we would rarely see him or any money. The longer he was out, the more relieved I was. Mother could spend time with my new brother with his deceased older brother's name. Apparently, that's important for babies. It's around that time when I learned how to pick pockets and get enough cash to pay for things like food. Some mothers would have been disappointed or enraged, but one of us had to take care of the family and it wasn't going to be her. She had children." I still don't personally condone a single thing I did.

"Did you send some money her way?"

"Of course, I did." I'm sure he just wants me to say it, but I'm not completely a monster. Even when my career took off, I remembered to send her some spending cash. That Lodskish guilt about children's duty to their parents runs deeper than I ever care to admit.

The biographer doesn't have a follow-up question, so I go on. "I'd say we had the same upbringing, but with him, Simon calmed down. At least, calmed down when he was home, and by that, I mean, he largely ignored his son. There must have been some guilt there, and Simon simply didn't trust himself."

I chuckle. "Piotrek's first words to me were asking about our father. The teenaged shithead I was told him about our other sibling. He needed to know." I laugh. "I remember the way he cried and yelled at me, calling me a witch because only a witch would tell such a horrible story." Unlike the other man in our family, he didn't use his fists against me. Instead, he beat his hands against his thighs in the gentlest way.

In some ways, Piotrek is right, but in others, I simply do not care. He has his life of office administration, reading, and interviews. He tells me about them sometimes during his visits to the prison. Sometimes he even calls. He has a voice mellow like peppermint tea and the kindest brown eyes I've ever seen. We might have been friends if things turned out differently. I wonder if I'm just another fascination for him. If I ask, he'll answer. But I don't want to ask.

"Is he wrong?" The biographer replies, having jotted down those notes. The recorder whirs next to us like a fourth companion.

I twist my face. "You know, maybe. I mean, witches cast magic and some of them aren't good. Heh. Maybe baby Piotrek was clairvoyant."

The biographer gently nods his head instead of responding. We both know Piotrek also has no magical abilities. At least, if he did, he never used them to any ends. I should ask him next time I see or hear from him.

"Though, I don't think I was really so bad, since that scary story made Piotrek work really, really hard to get out of Pier-Upon-Pier City. I mean, I did too, but my exit had consequences."

"I would imagine leaving to another town and cutting off ties has consequences."

I glare at him. I only fucked off to the other side of the West Gilson River. "You know exactly what I mean. His escape has *outcomes*. Unless he got into some really fancy crime and got hellaciously sloppy with it, then maybe I'd see him here. However, as far as I've heard, he's been a good kid." I never really learned what Piotrek got up to as far as his profession went. I only knew the dailies.

It got him close with the police, so it could be anything, really. But he never joined the force itself. He never carried a badge, fired a gun, or beat someone senseless with a baton. I can't tell if it makes him better or worse, but it makes me bitter because, well.

Piotrek is the reason I am within these four stone walls telling my life story to this over-curious stranger.

Then

We never had holidays in my home growing up, not really. Sure, Mother had the day off; she cooked some extra food. When she remembered the traditions, it would be a multi-piece meal full of fish and cream. No meat, but sometimes we didn't have the choice. Simon was drunk.

As a gift to myself, I would get special editions of my true crime rags. It was during the year's end holidays that I also got my first manga with stolen money. It was about a young boy using magic to become the leader of his village. It's still on-going. But I remember how the story of friendship, support, and evil's banishment gripped my heart.

If only the writer and artist learned that I would be one of the evils people sought to dispel.

As an adult, my idea of the holidays involved special nights at bars or restaurants, enjoying the company of other lonely people who didn't have families to go home to. At the same time, the holidays meant nothing to me, not really.

Frieda and I dated on and off during the eight years between us meeting and the year she invited me to the holidays at her family's house. We were in one of our on periods, where I spent most evenings at her house, lounging, enjoying new pay. She put most of her earnings into her food truck—she took her cover very seriously.

"So, my family throws this big holiday gathering every year and I was thinking: you should join me as my plus one."

"Are you sure?" I asked, lying on her chest as she stroked my brown hair.

"Yes, I'm positive. You don't look like you do crimes as your primary source of income. Plus, I might have mentioned you to my sister once or twice."

I clenched my jaw. I never gave her those permissions. "What does she know?"

"Nothing, Ruta-darling! Just that you're handsome and make me happy. She wants to meet you."

I broke my own tension with a smile. "Ah, should I bring anything?" Academically, I knew the holidays were for gift exchanges. Those last two weeks of the year were for an extended celebration of making it through another twelve months.

"Yes, they have a list. I have a copy somewhere." She made no movement to find it at that time. We simply lay there, cozy in our relationship, comfortable with ourselves. It was getting serious.

But a few days later, she shared the wish list with me. It was different stationery and home goods, things I knew I could get the finest available with the income I have. Frieda and I spent an entire afternoon in our panties wrapping presents and writing personalized notes. Frieda helped me double check the names and that the gifts corresponded with the notes. These activities ran into the evening. It was one of my favorite nights with her, though I couldn't quite explain why.

The party took place at a mansion in Westbingley. Frieda had a massive extended family—her sister's house proved the perfect location. Though it was the largest home I had ever seen, it was not even one of the largest on its block. We drove into a cul-de-sac lined with trees decorated in lights and bulbs. A wintery spirit blessed this place in ways that felt like I entered a different country altogether. This wasn't the gritty Benedicta of New Harbor and Pier-Upon-Pier City that I had known my whole life. These streets were full of decoration and cheer. Though clouds hung low in the sky, the evening maintained an air of enchantment. I didn't think I'd have any trouble with any Syndicate members, not that night.

Though we were among the last to arrive, we were greeted with more warmth than I could ever have mustered for myself. Even though I was a first-time guest, I got the same warm embrace from Frieda's sister, Alys. They shared a nose, thick brows, and a pleasant demeanor with Frieda. Aside from that, they were as different as siblings can be.

Alys had a nonbinary partner, with whom they shared two children. The home they lived in, however, had more rooms than necessary for four people. Each room had a different color pallete. I forget what they said they did for work, though. With the responsibilities of motherhood, I'm not sure the sister had a profession.

Though I had money, I considered myself rich, not wealthy. Wealthy meant owning land and having this level of excessive domesticity.

They even hired waitstaff to serve wine and hors d'oeuvres in the party's opening hours. There were small pastry parcels and meat on sticks and veggies dipped in various sauces. At this point in my life, I did well for myself. Some habits die hard, and I eat as if I had never been fed.

Where Frieda got her height from mystified me. No one in that room—not even the men—stood as tall as she did. It made her easy to find among the partygoers.

I dressed better for this affair. Instead of braiding my hair in its wreath, I let it hang in loose curls treated with heat and spray. For the first time in forever, I wore a dress. It had pointy shoulders and hugged my hips through my knees. Should anything go wrong, I would have to rip the seam on the side to allow for movement. I dared not wear heels. With the cold weather, boots proved a smarter choice anyway.

Frieda wore a large cape with a popped collar and wide-legged pants in a festive burgundy color. There would be no way for me to lose her among her over a dozen relatives and their partners and children.

I nursed a glass of bubbling wine in a corner. In this first living room, there was a grand piano near a vibrant fireplace. Family photos decorated the mantle. A tree stood tall, decorated so thoroughly, you wouldn't even know there was a tree beneath it. Holiday cheer, as I've said already, wasn't part of my being or upbringing. But I appreciated the art of it.

"Hi there, I see you're here as a partner." My resemblance to this young man struck me as uncanny. We have the same hooded brown eyes. The other facial features seem hand-picked from each of our parents. I was regretfully Simon's daughter, and he was definitely our mother's son. His hair was a dirty blonde in wild curls which he attempted to tame with hair product. It formed a bit of a crust in places—a stylistic choice that still beguiles me.

"Yes, I've never been to one of these," I said, tucking a stray strand behind my ear. My hand with the rings clicked the metal bands together. Only I could hear it over the music and din of lively conversation. It soothed me.

"My name is Piotrek Pawlak." He offered me his glass to clink.

My mind halted to a stop. "Pawlak? No way. That's my last name."

His jaw opened and closed a few times. "Your name isn't...Ruta by any chance?"

"It is! Wow." My eyes widened, and I hoped the flush over my face wasn't obvious.

Frieda saw the encounter. She kissed me on the cheek when she came over to us. "Don't look so nervous, darling. And who is this? I don't think I've seen him before."

"My name is Piotrek, I'm with Elisa." He tilted his chin toward this short, red-headed woman whose tawny skin shone against her deep green bubble dress. "We just had a wild moment, sorry."

"He's my brother," I mumbled, almost in a whisper.

"Darling, I couldn't catch that."

"He's my brother," I repeated, louder. The words rang fake like a bad key.

"Wow, this is holiday magic." She swiped her glass, some bubbly spilling out. "We should toast to that." Freckles danced on her cheeks when she drank. It was very charming, though it didn't distract me from my distress.

I deeply didn't want to toast to family. Much like Frieda's uncanny ability to know where I was, I wondered if it passed on among her relatives—whoever Piotrek came with had to know I was here. But if my maths were correct, Piotrek couldn't be older than twenty-five. How many of these affairs had he attended? Surely, it couldn't have been too many, but I didn't want to prolong the interaction to find out

This kind of familial love and enjoyment that permeated every other interaction in that house came too many years too late for me. I couldn't deny how much such a reunion and such camaraderie touched me. Tears pricked my eyes, and no one was allowed to see me cry, not even myself.

I excused myself, got my coat, and left with the pretense of smoking. I never even touched a cigarette, though prison has tempted me. Snow fell outside. The world was silent save for the cacophony inside, full of cheer that I had never experienced.

Frieda followed me. "Is everything all right, darling?"

I looked up at the clouded sky, trying to keep the tears in. It was futile. My cheeks got wet quickly. "This house is the last place I expected to see a family member. Sorry, I'm just...overwhelmed."

She wrapped me in her arms, in that way that made sure my face rested precisely under her chest. It was my comfort zone. I felt safe.

"Take as much time as you need," Frieda said before planting a kiss on the top of my head. "Well, that is, until dinner is served, but we have time."

"Aren't you cold?" Her rich fabric muffled my voice.

"Only if you are."

I never will be.

We stood like for about ten minutes before my face calmed enough to be seen among others again. I hated embarrassing myself, but it seemed unavoidable in that circumstance.

Because Alys coordinated the meal, the catering, and the dessert entertainment, they decided the seating arrangements. They made sure Frieda and I sat together. Piotrek and I were on opposite ends of the large dining table. For that, I was grateful. The children even had their own table. I was grateful for that too.

Throughout the hours of dinner, we ate our way through several dishes of various fish—some in oil, others in cream, others fried—and dumplings full of cabbage, mushrooms, potato, or any combination thereof. I drank my obligatory two drinks before switching to sparkling water and tea.

Before Frieda and I got in a car to go home, Piotrek wanted to exchange contact information. I brushed him aside, pretending that I didn't have a phone or an address. He ran away from home first; he could stay safe and far away from me until the end of his days if he wished. The way he argued with me suggested he didn't understand. I reminded him that I was a witch.

I remembered him saying, "Oh, that was me being silly as a child. I'm sure that's not the case anymore."

How monstrously wrong he would be.

Because I never kept in touch with anyone in that family, I was surprised that a courier found me with a note from Piotrek. All it said was that Simon left. That astonished me. The letter was several months old—I didn't make myself easy to find whatsoever—but I guess Simon didn't have anyone else to rail on when he got into his drunken rages. The letter mentioned Mother actually fighting back. Of course, she found the fight after she lost one child and didn't want to see another one perish. Of course, she found the fight once both her children had fled the nest. It surprised me that it was enough to drive him away. It pisses me off in that way where I wish she had fought back sooner, sparing us a whole lot of stress.

Piotrek's note also came with a gift: the name of Simon's new family.

It took me years to develop, but I finally had the magic and abilities needed to take down my father. It wasn't that I wanted to protect that other family. I didn't give a shit about them as people.

I needed permission.

I needed an excuse.

And I found one in the form of his new fresh terror in a family much larger than ours in a house that could appropriately be called such.

Even with several phonebooks at my disposal, it took a few days for me to find Simon's new family. It seemed that everyone named Pawlak was doomed to live and die in the trinity of states around Pier-Upon-Pier City. Simon's new rage depository settled in the Provisions State, in a quaint town called New Myristica, known for its nutmeg, named after a tree that grows halfway across the world.

I liked trailing people. Sitting in my car in observation gave me the opportunity to read the latest volumes of manga which I used my Syndicate earnings to keep up with. What? International tariffs made them incredibly expensive, and I wanted to support my favorite artists and storytellers.

From within that tidy vehicle, I observed Simon leaving his house only for him to enter it again. This happened several times. On my fourth stake out, two white men in tan suits but no recognizable uniform knocked on my window. I put down my manga and rolled it open. "Can I help you?"

"Your car has been parked here for days." The one speaking had a thick blonde beard and aviators on, like an asshole. The other one reminded me of an egg wearing aviators. His head glinted in the springtime sun.

"I wasn't aware that I needed a permit." There was no signage anywhere. New Myristica was painfully residential like that, with each house having a garage, and parking being first come first serve otherwise.

"You don't, but we've got questions."

The egg-shaped one cracked his knuckles in a fist.

I raised my hand. Time stopped around me. Since I had no intention of killing my father at that moment, I didn't wear gloves. I did the best I could with the gifts Frieda left me. I had a sandwich bag full of these tiny syringes filled with poison for emergencies. I grabbed one of them in a way that let me prick, plunge, and retreat in seconds. I leaned forward and pushed the needle onto the man's exposed hand. It takes a bit more contorting to get at the second one, but I succeeded without our skin even meeting. (I didn't want to risk him coming into my time frame.)

The poison started its dastardly chemical reaction once time returned to its standard cadence.

"Look gentlemen, I have nothing for you." I shrugged, knowing that they didn't see me reach for weapons. "If it makes you feel better, I will leave. You'll never see me again."

"Good." He took a few steps back.

The thing with this method of poisoning was that it acted quickly.

My tires were generic—the tracks would not lead the authorities to me. Plus, these men had guns on their hips, and in the Provisions State, you couldn't get away with carrying a weapon in the open like that without being in the right profession.

The egg man started frothing at the mouth first. Then the bearded one. They fell, gurgling. It sounded loud to me, but the commotion wasn't enough to summon any spectators. Or, out of an abundance of self-preservation, they didn't investigate for fear of getting involved in business worse than the deaths taking place.

It was a shame they fell so close to my car. My wheels bounced off their bodies with stomach-churning crunching sounds.

This surveillance wasn't supposed to get messy. Thankfully, I spent enough time studying Simon to know approximately how his schedule worked and when I could expect him to be going wherever it was that he went.

Now

"You just had to get in a pair of kills," the biographer murmurs. He thinks he's quiet, but I heard it. "Here I was beginning to think you weren't the monster people say you were."

I stop, jaw clenching. If we're going to get into technicalities and syntax, my father was the monster needing vanquishing. I disliked how long it took me to be that hero. For as satisfied as I was that it had been by my hand, I felt sadder that I didn't do it sooner. I didn't have the power years ago, but I wish I did. I wake up in the middle of the night sometimes, wondering why he got to live to such an old age.

If I acted sooner, we wouldn't have gotten the Piotrek who got to grow up and live a full life. Perhaps it might have been better for me to have prevented him from happening at all. Perhaps there would have only been the one Piotrek who didn't get a chance to go to school, since he died so young. This line of wondering is ultimately pointless.

"I can't be the monster," I say. "I'm the hero in this wretched tale."

The biographer takes off his square glasses to make sure I can see his widened, brown eyes. "You killed your father?" His voice shakes.

I don't know what he expects from talking to a violent criminal. "I'm getting there."

His throat bobs in a loud swallow as I continue.

Chapter 6: The Truth About My Father

Thirty-six years old

Then

I thought that one series of days would have been enough, but I could be wrong sometimes. The more I trailed my father, the more I unfortunately learned that he got a lot of his money by dropping "anonymous" tips to the police. These mistakes belonged to Ruta as a teen and young adult, not adult Ruta.

This new information, however, posed a danger to me specifically.

One of my primary needs related to keeping my brain constantly spinning with stories. So many new issues and chapters and volumes came out per month. The other need was that Frieda's desires got increasingly expensive. She wanted to go to the fancier clubs where the lights shone bright and the music vibrated from your feet to your head. Plus, the dinners and fashions became more elaborate.

Her time meant more to me than I will ever admit.

I worried so much about her that I forgot to do things for myself. Of course, I managed my bills, my contracts, and other arrangements. But self-care and personal treats fell by the wayside. I wasn't going to ask her to take on this job of eliminating my father, though her lack of relationship with him probably made her the more viable candidate for the hit. Whatever.

A darkness had been settling around Frieda. As if the walls were closing in around her, and, I supposed, they were. Simon trailed her but had no luck. Still, she had more erratic ideas: mass casualties. I shrugged them off as jokes until one day I learned of a sandwich-selling poisoner planning to eliminate an entire city by poisoning its reservoir.

I'll get into that later.

Simon didn't get anywhere near Frieda. The problem specifically arose when Simon got involved with a Syndicate rival of Ten Pan's while also being an informant for the police. He posed a big problem because if one Syndicate falls, the others follow shortly after. I had enough of a nest egg that if I wanted to quit working, I could. This wasn't about losing work—it was about avoiding prison.

I swear, it's funny now, but back then, it was a legitimate fear of mine—I was so young. So naive, so unsure of how anything worked.

I had plenty of self-motivation to take out my own father. I could have done it for free. Luckily, I didn't have to take matters into my own hands. Ten Pan set a dinner date with me at his grandmother's restaurant. It occurred to me then just how old he had gotten. Gray beard hairs outweighed the blonde. He shaved his head such that the stubble formed its own hair style. He didn't bother getting properly dressed. We ate with me in my killer's uniform and him in that awful tracksuit, which lost its sheen with age and shitty washing. (He had several of the same pair and each looked worse for wear.)

"I have a job for you—Simon Pawlak," he said. We each ate soup full of rye, eggs, and sausage. "He's causing me a bit of a problem."

"I'll get him out of your business," I replied. The soup smelled divine, especially in contrast to the roaring storm outside. "It's no problem."

"Are you okay with this, Icy?" he asked, something like concern coloring his face.

"Why wouldn't I be?" I shrugged and slurped my soup.

"You...your last name." His grin that split his face in half made me want to kill him at that table. It was annoying.

"Oh, I'm aware." It seemed silly for me to disclose that Simon was my father, but the relation is obvious. Pawlak wasn't the most common last name, especially in Benedicta.

"I'll up the pay, if you want." He didn't dare ask to move the hit onto someone else.

I chewed on an egg. "Please, that won't be necessary."

Like I said, I would kill my father for free.

The years had not been kind to Simon Pawlak. His hairline receded. He had the facial rash of someone lost in alcohol's haze. His pale brown eyes had that glazed-over look.

I would be stupid to think this an easy hit.

After a round of beers with his buddies in Pier-Upon-Pier City—not too far from my birthplace, actually—I found Simon stumbling through the streets. It was empty. A cool breeze came in from the West Gilson. There was no better time to strike.

I parked my dinky car several blocks behind him. Nothing suspicious. There were other cars, though there were no other patrons or late-night warriors. The wind was quiet—a perfect spring evening.

From within my glove compartment, I grabbed a syringe. Frieda taught me how much to use based on body weight, but truthfully, I injected as much as would be needed to slay a person. I labeled them, kept them organized. Because this was my father, I wanted to make sure he was over and done with in one movement. I had nothing dramatic to say to him—I rarely said anything to any of my targets. I'd grown efficient, and my father wasn't an exception.

With a shaky exhale, I collected myself and exited the car. Black leather gloves on, syringe in my hand, my dad was going to meet his e nd.

On quiet feet, I made my move against him. He didn't indicate that heard me approach.

As I poised to strike, he turned around and grabbed my wrist.

"Oh, I knew this was coming," Simon snarled. The crusty remains of tears spilled from his eyes.

Without saying a word, he threw me aside into the alleyway as if I weighed nothing. I managed to stay on my feet—I didn't give him the satisfaction of grounding me. I didn't know where this coordination and training could have come from. He's in his sixties, I should be able to deal with this easily.

But I couldn't. He came at me with the power and ferocity of a freight train. I barely dodged his clutches. The syringe fell on the darkened street. There was no recovering it. It was suspicious as fuck, but there was no way to link it to either of us.

I only hoped that I didn't step on it by accident.

Hand-to-hand combat was never in my repertoire. But a drunkard versus someone sober should have worked in my favor. Except it didn't. He ducked under my balled fists. His meaty hands clasped my neck. Simon killed one child and killing another one wasn't beneath him.

I had to stay focused. Instead of hitting him, I poured all my effort into freezing. Time, him, anything. Freezing him proved easiest, especially as my head grew light. Magic kept me present.

I grabbed his forearms and pushed as much ice as I could into his bare skin. My teeth scraped against each other as black spots formed in my vision.

He hissed. "What is this?"

I didn't respond. I never showed him my magic and he never grew his own proficiency.

With my vision faltering, his arms blackened around my palms like frostbite. He grunted in pain, one that I didn't think he was capable of experiencing for himself. No one ever fought back before. My mother did, but I don't think she caused him any harm or damage.

This violence would be his last.

Unable to bear the ice, he released me. I choked and breathed heavily, gulping at air as if given a second life. His fingers could not move. Red flushed against his face and in his eyes. Before I gave him another chance to pin me down, I grabbed his head. I siphoned as much ice magic into my hands as I could. Crystals formed along the skin of his forehead, covering his eyes. He screamed until frost covered his mouth, stopping his tongue.

Eventually, he stopped making any noise at all. I released him. He landed with a thud.

The clock struck midnight. It was my thirty-sixth birthday when I felled my father. Not sure if it was a gift or a curse, but I will never deny how good it felt.

Now

"Did it bring you closure?" the biographer asks while furiously scribbling the details of that murder. It isn't even the full story, but there's no way and no reason for him to know that.

I bob my head from side to side. Evaluating emotional fall-out isn't really a skill for me. I usually kill and commit crimes for tangible pay, not emotional consequence. It's a job to me, like sorting files at an office is for a secretary. There's no emotion attached—at least, I hoped there wasn't for lay people.

I sigh. "I suppose so. I don't have the right magic to bring Piotrek the First back, but it made me feel good knowing that there was some kind of retribution. You can't kill kids like that and then just...nothing?"

He adds a few notes. "Did you ever meet the new family?"

"Of course not. I didn't kill Simon for their sake." I still don't care about them. I hope they're doing decently. I glance over the tip of my nose. "This isn't going to the authorities, is it?"

"No, just confirming suspicions." His eyes widen for a second, but I sure catch it. Even, handcuffed, I am the scariest thing to this person. "There are rumors floating around that it was a Syndicate-sponsored hit."

I guffaw at that. "Please, Simon wasn't in the business of fucking over people more powerful than him or people he didn't know. I don't think Ten Pan wanted to confront me about my father directly." I never confirmed nor denied the connection. In fact, Ten Pan once told me that I sloughed off an iceberg because there is no way a person could be as cold as I am. I doubt Ten Pan cared at all about my relations.

The biographer asks, "The Syndicate runs off collateral and insurance policies. What did they have over you?"

God, this man is annoying. "Remind me: what am I in the can for?" I keep my gaze fixed on the steel table in front of me.

The biographer flips to other pages of his notes. "The charges here read five counts of murder and several more counts of attempted murder."

I keep my face still at the word *attempted*. They just couldn't prove it was me. If there is a death associated with Ten Pan, it was likely me.

"The Syndicates also have their talons in the police force, yeah?" I continue. "If they wanted me gone, they just needed to snap their fingers."

"And was it a snap that landed you here?"

It annoys me how well this biographer catches me on my own turns of phrase. This one elicits a smile anyway. "I'm getting there, buddy."

Chapter 7: Love's End

Thirty-seven years old

Then

The joyous jingle of a food truck coming through the neighborhood will forever set off tears.

Shortly after dispatching my father, I followed up on the poisoner rumor, which I hated getting from Ten Pan. I wondered if I would have taken it better if Frieda told me herself. She hated her hometown on the outskirts of New Harbor in Westbingley. This I knew. But we should have talked about the lines we drew as far as our work went. I only went after specific targets, with names and indictments that the city simply was too cowardly or money-hungry to do anything about. No children, and no parents killed in front of their children.

Having a code doesn't make me having the drive to stop Frieda right or righteous or whatever heroic adjective you want to put on it. But it felt good and right to me. With no hope for my own future and too many lives taken for a cheerful ending, I still had my standards.

The fact that I was the only one capable of stopping Frieda also made it clear that a happy ending was not for me to hope for.

The jingle for her food truck resounded off the trees with garbled speed. She didn't call out for her signature fresh mutton. Instead, she raced down the forested roads to her hometown.

I stood in the middle of the highway, sweating, panting. Even in frozen time, my body took on all the pain and effort of running fast enough to stop a truck. It was the only way I could have caught up without speeding away in a vehicle of my own. Best not to get highway patrolman involved in a lover's spat between contract killers.

Frieda rolled down her window and hollered to me. "Darling, what are you doing? I'm going to run you over, get off the road."

"I can't...I can't let you through." Panting punctuated my syllables. Sweat poured down my face like rain even though the sun shone perfectly. I couldn't even face her. I bent over, hands holding the rest of my body up.

"But you don't understand, they have to die." Her voice cracked like ice in a way I never heard it before.

I wasn't going to let Frieda poison innocent people because of her own unhinged agitation. "I'm sure they do, trust me. But those people haven't done anything."

Frieda slapped her horn. It blared and echoed through the trees. " *Those people* are my family. They have what I don't! I'm sick of being beholden to them, Icy. I'm sick of being less than, a burden to the rest of them."

She never called me by some frost-related nickname until that moment. She never mentioned harboring any resentment towards the normal life her sister led. It hurt so much. It hurt like I had never known Frieda at all. If she wanted to thoroughly break my heart, she succeeded. Instead of focusing on my rage, I remained fixated on preventing unnecessary collateral damage.

"I'm not letting you do this." My voice cracked. I sounded like the world's most pathetic frog.

"Suit yourself!" Frieda revved the engine. She really was about to run me over.

I didn't want it to end with her life in my hands, but she left me no choice. Breathing was hard. My heart ached in a way it never had.

Despite my exhaustion, my magic reserves outweighed my physical abilities. I raised my arm and channeled into the depths of my magical capacity. Pushing the metaphysical net out, I enveloped myself and Frieda. The wheels made one rotation, but it wasn't enough to propel the car towards me. I caught it in time.

I hopped onto the food truck's hood. With one part of my mind focused on maintaining time's stillness, I let another piece summon ice and wrap it around Frieda's still-beating heart. In frozen time, it doesn't beat. I needed it to stop long enough for brain death. I wanted her death to be as swift and painless as it could be.

I stayed still, freezing her blood for fifteen minutes. Time melted back into motion around me as my own vision blackened.

The last thing Frieda saw before slumping forward onto her horn was me laying my hands over her. Tears streamed down my face, freezing as I cast. It was, painfully, enough.

Ten years to the day Frieda and I met, our relationship ended for good.

What I Didn't Tell the Biographer - Grief

I wept so hard.

When time returned to its established pace, blood flowed out of Frieda's mouth and nose. My hands were not the steadiest while wrapping her heart in a cocoon of ice. Shards pierced its pericardium and cut into the arteries and made a whole mess inside. Someone was going to find the body and it wouldn't look like a heart attack. I had been so careless, but I couldn't let Frieda destroy so many lives. If she wanted to kill her sister and entire family, she could have just done it without involving anyone else. She could have just gone to their home, given them some poison, and the coroner would declare it all the strangest family heart attack.

I would not have helped her.

I would have tried to talk her out of it, but knowing that she jumped straight to eliminating the entire town and told fucking Ten Pan about it...I couldn't pretend I didn't know of her plans.

I killed Frieda in the name of a town whose name I never got.

When I hopped off the truck, I wept with a ferocity I worried would rupture my lungs. I almost wished it worked like that.

Killing Frieda and having Ten Pan pay me as if he ordered the hit confirmed one thing: the man needed to go.

And if it got me put in prison, so be it.

Chapter 8: Severance

Thirty-eight years old

Now

"And how did killing Frieda make you feel?"

I want to jump across the table and bite that biographer's nose off with frost. How the fuck did he think it made me feel? It felt bad just recounting the sordid affair. My heart is thundering through my ears, and I can barely see anything beyond how angry I fucking am. Frieda should have calmed the fuck down instead of going full villain out of jealousy. Maybe I didn't have to kill her, but if even *she* turned to ice-based insults and literally no brakes, there's nothing kinder I could have done.

"Felt bad, you know?" It was the only right answer.

"So, there were rumors that Ten Pan paid you to kill off Frieda. They said it was because she was encroaching on his territory, getting too close..."

I didn't hear the rest of what he said. My blood started to boil, and I didn't think it was possible. I never took the money from Ten Pan. I think it's what started our rift *because how dare he*. There was no way for him to have known about our connection, however, he should have noticed the change in my M.O. No longer only ice-killings, but also poison. If he were at all a good employer, he'd have paid attention. In addition to being a bastard, Ten Pan was also a terrible manager.

I'm not sure how long the biographer talks, but I interrupt him with, "You're really starting to annoy me."

"Repeat that?" the biographer says.

The words aren't supposed to leave my mouth. "Fuck. I mean, I don't know what the rumors were. But the fact that Ten Pan had a hand in it made me really uneasy, you know?"

"And how would you describe that unease?"

If any violence befalls this hapless, senseless individual, remember: he's the one who asked for it.

I groan, grinding my teeth. The unease in this room feels like critters underneath my skin. "I don't think he and I ever trusted each other. But I signed every contract in literal blood. They were extremely dangerous, both physically and reputationally. His word could mean I never work again. A whisper in the right ear gets me put away. My only options were to perform perfectly and never get caught."

"He wasn't the one who sold you out, though." The biographer sucks in his lips, realizing how bone-headed his statement is.

If you've read the news, it is no secret who sold me out. Yes, I should have tapped into my normal level of paranoid carefulness. But Piotrek meant no one any harm, and to this day, I believe him. No one got hurt in the way he coordinated my take down. Besides, prison has been disturbingly comfortable. There's structure. I haven't committed the kinds of crimes that make me a victim of further violence. I keep to myself. Life here is okay, all things considered.

But this biographer wants to know about Piotrek, which feels a little problematic. But if he wants to know, then I'll tell him.

"I guess we are going there." I chuckle. This story pisses me off so much.

Then

With Frieda gone, I had no interest in connecting with her family. Not with the knowledge that I had eliminated her. They would ask me how I was coping and the word vomit of how she tried to *kill them all* would come tumbling out. No one needed that mess. I especially didn't need that mess.

So, I avoided them.

I also avoided Ten Pan on non-contract conversations. I couldn't trust him to keep me together or safe. My personal connections had gone from two to zero, and I didn't know what to do with that isolation and loneliness.

As if someone told him about my fatal personal problems, Piotrek found me again via courier. In that letter, he told me he heard Simon died of "a brain hemorrhage." He didn't know who I was, really, or that I had ice magic, so he said it shocked him. He mentioned that it made him remember the virtues of family. Because of that strange guilt, he wants to reconnect.

Or, really, connect for the first time.

The fact that we met as adults could offer an opportunity for a relationship unmarred by childish insults or growing pains. We could move beyond having to process trauma we didn't share from parents who technically raised us.

I made the courier wait as I drafted a response.

The courier received a letter from me to Piotrek inviting him out to a loud bar where we could talk about anything and everything, drowned out by the noise. Neither of us would have to get dressed up. It's far away from my home in Pier-Upon-Pier City, so I'm not shitting where I eat. If the meal goes disastrously, I never have to go back.

It was in one of the new residential areas of Central Isle. Apartment complexes towered over historical town homes converted into these commercial hubs. I enjoyed the atmosphere despite the cost to New Harbor's spirit. Sometimes the aesthetic was bad, but in others, it was charming. No wonder the city transformed considerably in my lifetime.

Inside, electronic music blared through the speakers. No one danced, all seated and swaying because the seats were too high. Plastic candles served as the primary light sources. Piotrek got there before me. He sat at an elevated table in the corner. He wore a pair of jeans and a loose tee shirt that made him look more like a college student than someone who's got his shit together. I was surprised the bouncers allowed him in.

I ordered two ciders and brought them over.

He thanked me, and we exchanged pleasantries. I wasn't sure how to hold that conversation, so he started. He told me of boarding school, his desk job, his healthy relationship with Elisa, and more. I kept quiet, mostly listening to how our same parents produced two very different people.

After one pint of cider, he ordered another. Clearly, he steeled himself for the real conversation to come. In my gut, I assumed there was an ulterior motive. No one just wanted to *talk* to me, and maybe that was why I turned out the way I did.

"I just need someone who can, you know." He turned his head sheepishly, leg bouncing against the floor as if he wanted to drill a hole through the tile. "Take care of a problem for me."

I raised a manicured brow. "A problem? What kind of problem?" The boy had money; I couldn't see what he needed me for. Most problems could be solved by throwing money at them.

"Um." He paled, but I waited patiently for him to continue. "The problem is that someone needs to go away. But I need someone who can, you know, actually do it."

I sucked in my lips. "I see." So, he did know what I did. I wonder if he learned it from Simon or from his other contacts.

"I'm...I'm willing to pay! I'm just..."

"Too much of a coward to solve your own problems?" I smirked to let him know that he should keep that softness. Taking lives shouldn't come as easily to anyone as easily as it came to me. "Look, buddy, name your price, and it's done. I just need the goods." Frieda was dead and could no longer provide me with poison.

"Goods..." The words trailed off into a deep bass line. I wasn't saying it explicitly or out loud. His head perked up after a few moments. "Ah, yes. I have a source. I can bring it to you if you'd like."

"Sounds good to me." We arranged a place and time.

We shook hands. It was the most familial gesture we ever engaged in.

———————————— ❄ ————————————

Weeks passed since my last kill, and it shamed me to think I would itch for it again. It wasn't even Frieda, but some asshole who owed Ten Pan money. It was easy, too easy, and grief stole whatever joy I could have gotten from the subsequent book purchases. I should have figured out a way of processing those feelings, but with my upbringing, therapy wasn't a consideration. Not sure it would have helped; too many bodies had gone cold by my hand for therapy to do anything meaningful.

At the appointed time, I parked behind a fast-food restaurant in the dead of night on a weekday. No one should be coming here. It's that liminal hour when those who worked too early were already starting their days and those who worked too late were already tucked into bed. It was just going to be me and my brother. Piotrek would bring the poison and his victim. I would freeze time, eliminate the target, take the cash, and move on.

Maybe I'd let Piotrek deeper into my life. Or not. I hadn't decided. The fact that he reached out to me for a job made me feel a certain wariness. He didn't want to get to know me—he wanted to use me. Which I can respect. Business is business, after all. But the simple cruelty of the pretense stung. There was no balm for it.

A car pulled into the lot. It was a common make, navy-colored number. The headlights blinded me; I raised a hand so I could see the driver better.

It was Piotrek. He arrived alone. Or so I thought. Something wasn't right. I unclicked my belt and get out to meet him. Before I had a chance to call out his name, more lights blinded me.

"Hands where we can see them," a high-pitched voice called. Dozens of people in uniforms emerged from behind the dumpster. I hadn't seen them upon entering. I cursed repeatedly.

This was a trap, and I walked far too easily into it.

I raised my hands. They fired at me with tasers before I had the chance to freeze time, freeze them, stop anything. I fell to the ground, writhing. I hoped my poisonings hurt less than that. Even to this day, I see sparks, and it sends me into a mild panic.

I was arrested for the distribution of illegal substances, the murder of those suits knocking on my window when I stalked my father, and the five murders all linked to Ten Pan.

What I Didn't Tell the Biographer - Who Killed Ten Pan

Of course, I killed Ten Pan. It's the last favor I ever did him.

I was a menace, sure, but him even more so. The more I learned about the Syndicates, the more I learned that he was all hot air. He even got cut out of deals because his temper got the better of him. Remember: he had periods of activity and rest, like a fucking bear.

He invited me out to the beach south of Pier-Upon-Pier City in the middle of the night after a final dinner at his grandmother's. He never got sauced there, mostly out of respect for her. He ate little, and his eyes bulged in an excitement unbecoming of the man.

The location, the time, the isolation—he meant to be rid of me.

He made me get rid of Frieda, of my father, of his exes. There was no one left to cause him problems except for the one who solved so many for him.

With this knowledge, I got dressed in my execution best: sapphire blue velour blazer, matching high-waisted shorts, black thigh-high boots, black gloves, and a small black purse for my last poison syringe—my last gift from Frieda. I love how it would be used against the man who tipped me off about her madness. The man who *paid me* for putting her to rest, the prick.

I took the night bus through Pier-Upon-Pier City's warehouse-lined streets in the beach-side district. Large lots full of shipping containers. Growling machines lifted them and set them down on top of each other. There wasn't a soul in sight. It was strange how much things have changed in thirty years. My mother wouldn't be working here anymore—it was all replaced by machines and people who knew how to take care of them.

The bus stopped almost an hour later at a boardwalk. Rickety stairs led to the murmuring sea beneath a starless sky. A cool, autumn wind blew from those bottomless waters. Somewhere down south, a storm raged. Maybe it would make it this far north, but I sincerely hoped not. If only my magic extended that far.

Silhouetted against the sweeping waves, I saw Ten Pan.

"Hey, Icy!" His voice carried over the rush of water. "Thanks for meeting me."

He was wearing the track suit. His feral eyes almost glowed in the nighttime light. Perhaps I was being paranoid. The moon hung in the sky, but he definitely resembled himself. If he was some kind of lunatic, it had nothing to do with physical transformation.

Nothing suggested those still existed, but my first ever paid hit was a vampire—anything was possible in this strange country of Benedicta.

My feet sank into the cold, wet sand as I approached him. These shoes would need a good scrub when I got home.

He lifted his hand. There was a gun. "It's been a pleasure working with you, Icy."

Before he had a chance to fire, I summoned magic, and the world stilled around us. The waves stopped mid-crash. Water droplets hung in the air. His hand held the gun, his finger not quite on the trigger. I didn't doubt for a moment that Ten Pan would have shot me in the head and been done with it. Clearly, it was his intention. But I never told him about the time magic.

I took the syringe out of my purse. Without hesitating even a little bit, I plunged it behind his ear, making sure it went right to his head. No risks with Ten Pan. If I tried to magic him dead without any support from more immediate murder methods, he would have killed me.

With this simple act, I beat him. No more payments, functionally fired, but that was fine for me.

Time unfroze long enough for me to get behind him. Before he realized what I'd done, the poison activated in his blood. His stomach curdled. He dropped the gun into the ocean and fell to his knees. Familiar white foam bubbled from his lips.

I smiled. That dead man couldn't see it.

The stress melted off my body, but there remained the issue of disposal. Leaving him to the sea proved too risky. The body could come back and spark an investigation.

I remembered Frieda's freezer in Ceramic Bay. The purse still held the key.

My magic was powerful. Freezing time proved more useful than simply creating ice anywhere else. I crouched and hoisted Ten Pan's corpse over my shoulder. I carried him back to the boardwalk, hoping a bus or other midnight beach goer didn't join me.

Cars lined a section of the boardwalk. I "borrowed" the dinkiest one I saw and drove through a time-stopped slipstream all the way to Ceramic Bay. No one saw it, not that I could tell. Ten Pan looked like he was taking a drunken nap in the backseat.

This was fine, all under control. Years ago, when Frieda taught me about poison, she showed me her facility. Unfortunately for me, it wasn't anywhere close to us in these wilds of the State of Piers; I had to drive across two bridges to get there.

None of the freezers were large or empty enough for Ten Pan's physique without having to butcher him. I didn't want to displace the mutton there since it would unfreeze and rot and cause a scene—not so fresh after all.

With time standing still, I worked carefully. Bones snapped and blood oozed through the tears in his skin. His tacky track suit caught most of the ick. I used the towels Frieda left behind to make sure the blood got sopped up and off the floor.

With some geometric manipulation, he was safely tucked away in that cold, mechanical coffin for years.

Just last month, they found him. Someone complained about odd smells. There was no one alive to pay the utility bills. I'm impressed and unsurprised that it took the authorities as many years as it did to finally find him.

Chapter 9: The Last Interview

Forty-five years old

Now

"Do you feel any animosity towards Piotrek? His betrayal must have hurt," the biographer says, projecting his own feelings onto my actions and motivations. It's unwise. We are not the same.

He booked time for one final session, and I am glad to be rid of him. I've run out of stories; he has enough for a compelling enough volume.

I lift my chin, crane my head back. "I'm not surprised though. Violence comes in cycles, and someone has to break the wheel." It was never going to be me. Violence got me to many of life's little and grander pleasures.

The biographer jots that down. It's not even that profound a metaphor. "Piotrek Pawlak became a prosecutor determined to take down the Syndicates."

I scoff. I don't read the news. "How's that working out for him?"

"Pretty decently. Though the power vacuums are..." He exhales. "Well, Ten Pan is certainly inactive." The biographer pulls out a folder of news articles.

"I can't read those, you know." I shake my shackles; the text is too far and small for me to parse.

The biographer turns to the bored guard behind him. The guard shakes their head, not allowing me to become unshackled to read news of my own family.

Gulping, the biographer stands. He pushes the folders towards me as if approaching a rabid dog. There is nothing I can do to harm him.

"Tell me when to flip," he says.

I lean forward, reading carefully. The first headline is about Piotrek and how he took down several Syndicate leaders. Violence erupted in their quiet neighborhoods because power in title isn't enough for some people.

"Next," I tell the biographer.

It shows a picture of Frieda's preparation station corded off with police tape. The authorities carry out several freezers. It names her with a last name I don't recognize. Masters, unsurprisingly, was a pseudonym. I cannot imagine how this revelation hits her family. Alys and her partner were such nice people.

And all I can think about is how lucky they are to be spared from Frieda's jealous rage spiral.

"Wow," I say, simply. They found the freezer. They found so many of Frieda's victims. She was more prolific than I could ever hope to be. I never asked her, but I had a feeling that she really wanted to stay in food service. It's such a volatile market and having any kind of financial security is a pipe dream. She kept herself afloat with crime, and honestly, I could not blame her.

That all being said, her sandwiches were good. She never gave me the recipe. It died with her.

"So, was it Frieda?" The biographer asks.

I shrug. "That sure is a question, isn't it?"

"So, you don't know." It's not a question.

As if it's a buoy, he closes the folders and pulls them back towards him. It reminds me more of a child reaching for a stuffed animal for comfort. This asshole has no idea what he's in for.

We spend much of the last hour clarifying smaller details.

"I hope you got everything you needed," I tell the biographer. "I'm not sure how much more I have left in me." I'm tired. My bones ache.

But that familiar coldness floods my fingers. I keep my face preternaturally still. I can't let him or the guards know what is happening. Did someone forget to drug my water? It didn't taste any differently. Something changed within my body. My bleeding had been excessive the last several weeks, but I didn't think it would have affected my magic.

An excitement I hadn't felt in decades thrills me.

"I think I have enough. Unfortunately for both of us, it might require some follow-ups." He rises and straightens his checkered shirt.

"You're so annoying," I grumble, eyes fixed on this shithead.

Power floods into my hands. I don't want to freeze him. I want to cast that net one last time. Magic's tendrils hover around me, filling that interview space.

Time freezes.

I push more ice magic through my wrists, making my shackles brittle enough to break.

In an orange jumpsuit, I leave to go back to my shoddy one-bedroom apartment and track down the volumes I came to love. My killing days are behind me.

I want to retire in peace away from everyone and anyone.

Additional Reading & Listening

If you enjoyed this novella and want to delve into what broke my fixations enough to pull this story together, please consider reading or listening to the following:

- *The Ice Man: Confessions of a Mafia Contract Killer* by Philip Carlo (2006, St. Martin's Press)

- *Last Call: A True Story of Love, Lust, and Murder in Queer New York* by Elon Green (2021, Celadon Press)

- Last Podcast on the Left's Three Part Series on Richard Kuklinski

  - Episode 326: Richard Kuklinski Part I – Origins of the Iceman

  - Episode 327: Richard Kuklinski Part II – Tales of the Iceman

  - Episode 328: Richard Kuklinski Part III – The Fall of the Iceman

Acknowledgments

The actual writing of a book is a solitary activity. Putting a book together to share with others—now *that's* a group effort. And I'm eternally grateful to the following individuals:

To James and Noah Feeman for their encouragement, early reading, editorial advice, and ineffable support of this project from when I thought I still wanted to pursue a traditional path to now.

To Kimberly Black for beta reading and helping me get a better handle of the descriptions of this reimagining of New York's tri-state area.

To Francesca Tacchi for their sensitivity reading regarding the depiction of the mafia.

To K.M. Enright for copy-editing, catching misplaced commas and continuity errors, and for the incredible cheerleading.

To Miloh E. Gorgevska for loving Ruta at first sight and for all your support in getting this project off the ground.

To everyone who blurbed and reviewed—thank you for the kind words and excitement, and for enjoying reading this story as much as I did writing it.

Finally, I want to thank my boyfriend, Matthew, for dealing with me through all the brain worms and supporting me as both a writer and being.

About the Author

Ladz was born in Poland, raised in New York City, and currently lives in Texas. When they're not a marketing manager for a major digital publisher, they're writing dark fantasy that tends to straddle other genres like true crime and horror. They have been a panelist at the 2020 Nebulas Conference, 2021 Weeknight Writers Exploring Story Structure Event, 2019 & 2021 Sirens Conference, and Discon III in 2021. They can be found online at jowritesfantasy.me or on Twitter/Instagram @ladzwriting.

Robot Dinosaur Press features queer, inclusive science fiction, fantasy, and horror books from a collective of global authors. For an introduction to our work, sign up to our newsletter at robotdinosaurpress.com/newsletter and receive a free anthology of short stories by RDP authors.

Also from Robot Dinosaur Press

The Peridot Shift by R J Theodore

In this Science Fantasy trilogy, a scrappy group of outsiders take a job to salvage some old ring from Peridot's gravity-caught garbage layer, and land squarely in the middle of a plot to take over (and possibly destroy) what's left of the already tormented planet.

The Phantom Traveler by R J Theodore

When one of Ehli's bantam sisters turns up dead, she tries to figure out what happened before she's blamed for the murder, and before the real killer strikes again.

The Wolf Among The Wild Hunt by Merc Fenn Wolfmoor

When a knight mistakenly kills a corrupted nun, he has one chance to redeem himself. He must run with the Wild Hunt: an age-old trial of blood and courage, where every step hides peril and carnage. Few have ever returned from the fae-haunted land...for in the Wild Hunt, you run or you die.

The Midnight Games: Six Stories About Games You Play Once edited by Rhiannon Rasmussen

An anthology featuring six frightening tales illustrated by Andrey Garin await you inside, with step by step instructions for those brave—or desperate—enough to play.

Sanctuary by Andi C. Buchanan

Morgan's home is a sanctuary for ghosts. When it is threatened they must fight for the queer, neurodivergent found-family they love and the home they've created.

Hero's Choice by Merc Fenn Wolfmoor

Never get between a Dark Lord and his son. Who needs destiny when you've got family?

They Dreamed of Dead Ships by Byron M. Kain

A terrifying plague sweeps the world, and there is nowhere safe...for it comes to you in a dream about a ship. And then it is too late.

A Starbound Solstice by Juliet Kemp

Celebrations, aliens, mistletoe, and a dangerous incident in the depths of mid-space. A sweet festive season space story with a touch of (queer) romance.

Friends For Robots: Short Stories by Merc Fenn Wolfmoor

An upbeat collection of short science fiction and fantasy stories featuring many good robots and their friends!

Unlikely Wonders edited by Juliet Kemp

An exciting collection of short Science Fiction and Fantasy stories from a stellar group of Robot Dinosaur Press authors

The Seritarchus by Novae Caelum

Homaj Rhialden never expected to rule the kingdom. But his father is dead, his older sibling the Heir is missing, and everyone he trusts is suspect. *The Seritarchus* is a standalone prequel serial to *The Stars and Green Magics*, with a genderfluid lead, MANY nonbinary characters, and lots of cloak and daggery court intrigue!

Good Monsters And Friends: Stories by Merc Fenn Wolfmoor

Making friends with monsters is easy—bring them cookies! In this collection of 33 tiny stories: A young man must find a new reality to live in when his disappear;. birds team up to right the wrongs of classic literature; an android raises baby dinosaurs after the human world ends; Grandma reveals how she invented intergalactic diplomacy...and more!

You Fed Us To the Roses by Carlie St. George

Final girls who team up. Dead boys still breathing. Ghosts who whisper secrets. Angels beyond the grave, yet not of heaven. Wolves who wear human skins. Ten disturbing, visceral, stories no horror fan will want to miss.

Banshees & Boba by Nia Quinn

I'm Gemma: witch and single mom to a twelve-year-old sass bucket. When my corporate job gives me the heave-ho, I decide it's time to try something new. Dragon manicurist? Golem artificer? How about monster-fighting mercenary? Have sword, will vanquish. Only my new job isn't quite what I was expecting it to be . . . I'm too young for a midlife crisis–aren't I?

The Truthspoken Heir: The Stars and Green Magics Season One by Novae Caelum

Two shapeshifting heirs, one interstellar kingdom. When royals can be anyone else including each other, who will rule? *The Stars and Green Magics* is an unabashed space fantasy serial with shapeshifting royals, vicious politics, complex aliens, and queerness everywhere! *The Truthspoken Heir* collects the complete first season.

<u>Magnificent: A Nonbinary Superhero Novella</u> by Novae Caelum

The world wants me to be a "normal" hero, but I'm genderqueer, and I'm never going to fit into their molds. So how do you save the world when you're just trying to figure out who you are?

www.ingramcontent.com/pod-product-compliance
Ingram Content Group UK Ltd.
Pitfield, Milton Keynes, MK11 3LW, UK
UKHW021347280125
4333UKWH00023B/162

9 781949 936650